Stone Mad

TOR BOOKS BY ELIZABETH BEAR

STONE MAD

ELIZABETH BEAR

A TOM DOHERTY ASSOCIATES BOOK

NEW YORK

STONE MAD

Copyright © 2018 by Sarah Wishnevsky Lynch

Cover illustration by Micah Epstein
Cover design by Christine Foltzer

Edited by Beth Meacham

A Tor.com Book
Published by Tom Doherty Associates
175 Fifth Avenue
New York, NY 10010

www.tor.com

Tor® is a registered trademark of
Macmillan Publishing Group, LLC.

ISBN 978-1-250-16382-0 (ebook)
ISBN 978-1-250-16383-7 (trade paperback)

First edition: March 2018

This book is for Arkady and Viv:
may you find your happily ever after!

Acknowledgments and Author's Note

Thank you, dear readers, for joining me on another adventure with Karen and Priya. Without your attention, they wouldn't have the existence they do. Suffice it to say, we are all very grateful.

It takes a village to make a book, but I'd like to acknowledge a few people in particular: my husband, Scott, who knows when to slide flat food under the door; my agent, Jennifer Jackson; her assistant, Michael Curry; my editors, Beth Meacham and Carl Engle-Laird; Jen Gunnels, capable interlocutor and organizer; Karl Gold, the production manager, and Lauren Hougen, the production editor, for keeping all the pieces together; the phenomenal copyediting of Barbara Wild and equally phenomenal proofreader Kyle Avery; Mordicai Knode and Katharine Duckett, and their much appreciated respective efforts in marketing and publicity; Peter Lutjen, for the beautiful cover design; and Micah Epstein, for the amazing cover art. Thank you, everyone!

I'd like to acknowledge the folks in my network who offered moral support during a personally and politically challenging time while this book was being written: my mother, Beth, Julia, Asha, Sarah, Fran, Celia, Jamie, Amanda, Amber, Alex, Devin, Arkady, Viv, Chelsea, Stella, Jodi, Fade, Max, Amal, Gretchen, Stephen, and Liz: thanks for helping keep my head above water.

I'd also like to thank my Patreon Patrons at the acknowledgment level: Jason Teakle, Graeme Wiliams, Clare Gmur, Brad Roberts, Maya Chhabra, Sharis Ingram, Inksea, Barb Kanyak, D Franklin, Max Kaehn, B. C. Brugger, Sara Hiat, John Appel, Jack Vickery, Emily Richards, Brigid Cain-O'Connor, Justin G. Wallace, Fred Yost, Edmund Schweppe, Wynne Tegyn, Batwrangler, Hisham El-Far, Noah Richards, Cathy B. Lannom, Brooks Moses, Kelly Brennan, Emily Gladstone Cole, Heather K., Tiff, Jenna Kass, Jack Gulick, and Mur Lafferty—thanks again for contributing to keeping the kittens housed and fed!

Stone Mad

No roach ain't never gonna run 'cross a flimflam man's plate, excepting the grifter in question's already got himself around the best part of his supper.

I know that. And I have known it since I was twelve years old. So it would have made me suspicious right off when the table to me and Priya's left started rocking against the floor to the sound of thumps and knocking just as their dessert was being cleared. Would have made me suspicious, that is, excepting I was already suspicious. I'd made my mind up about the two redheaded young ladies inhabiting that table within fifteen minutes of them sitting down next to us, and decided I knew what sort of rookery they was like to play.

You know and I know that deciding you know something when you don't is about the deadliest thing a person can do. Yet what does everybody under God's blue sky keep right on to doing?

It takes front to pull off a free-meal swindle, and I'm an admirer of gall. And the ladies at the thumping table had gall, in spades, a royal flush of it. Because it weren't just a roach from out their sleeve that they was producing, but a whole simulation of a haunting, and right out in the middle of the formal dining room at the Rain City Riverside Hotel, which was aglitter with newfangled electric lights and ringing with crystal, being the finest establishment of its or any kind in Rapid City.

If I, Karen Memery, was taking my best girl out to celebrate the best day of our lives I weren't not going to take her to cream gravy!

That was one reason I was plumb undecided about what to do about those table thumpers. I didn't want to ruin our dinner, you see.

And then there was a slim possibility I was wrong about them girls, and the haint was legitimate. It was a good scheme they had going, because of course there's rumors the Riverside is haunted even though there ain't never been but the one single massacre in it, and what's a frontier hotel without a massacre or two? You need at least one to be going on with before you can call yourself a proper elbow-bending joint, closer to three if you're going to run a gaming parlor.

There was an Unpleasant Incident some years back, before I came to town, where a miner back from Alaska went crazy and killed a whole piano parlor full of people, including himself. Well, he's supposed to only have blinded the piano player. The Professor, who plays piano at the Hôtel Ma Cherie, told me he knew the blinded man himself and had it straight from his own mouth.

But if I weren't wrong about 'em, well. I was involved in the hospitality industry, as you might call it, for long enough to know how hard it can be to keep such a business running, even in a gold rush town like Rapid City. Dining halls run on real small margins, even fancy ones, and free dinner specialists can run them out of business right quick.

But then on the other other other hand, you mind when I say "ladies" that those girls was the same kind of ladies as Priya and me. Which is to say West-Coast Ladies, Doves of the Settlement, or, as you like. Seamstresses, which is what the city taxed us as, and what I would have written on my Census form if I'd still been doing it next year coming up, which was fixing to be 1880 unless something unexpected happened: "Karen Memery, Seamstress, Orphan, Age 17."

Ladies maybe not of the evening, but definitely ladies of the demimondaine, to turn a phrase like my friend Beatrice would.

So I was, as you might call it, conflicted.

———————

Priya and me was out to celebrate spending the reward money we'd earned by being heroes and genuine deputized U.S. Marshals. I was just about over my pneumonia, and my hip only pained me when it rained—which in Rapid City was, to be sure, almost all of the time.

But I was working on gaining back some of the weight I'd lost, and we'd bought us a tidy modest outfit with a barn and some pasturage and a kitchen without even a hand pump indoors, and an old-fashioned Franklin stove—not one of those modern self-cookers like Miss Lizzie is making a killing off building for the rich people's houses. It was a sweet little place that would be a tinker shop for Priya and a dude ranch and breaking stable for me. I was taking her out to dinner and she was taking me out to a magic show, both at the Rain City Riverside Hotel, where the widow of the famous late illusionist Micajah Horner was meant to be demonstrating a selection of his tricks.

We got our share of stares, two ladies on our own, and Priya in trousers, though I tried not to take it personal. Maybe everybody was just staring because we was the heroes what had saved the town that winter previous with no more to work with than a house full of lightskirts and a Singer sewing machine.

That big Singer that Priya had turned into a suit of battle armor was back in our barn, and it still sewed, in spite of everything. If I couldn't make a living breaking horses, I could always be a modiste.

Us being temporarily famous might have been the source of the fuss, honest, because after we disembarked from a steam carriage that bore a striking resemblance to a horseless, burnished-steel version of Cinderella's pumpkin, the maître d'hôtel had welcomed us inside effusively before showing us to the best two-top in the house. His name was Alexandre, and he was a tall, narrow, elegant Negro Frenchman in an evening suit. He was French French, not New Orleans French, and he was the pride and joy of the Rain City Riverside Hotel dining room.

The dining room is French, and everybody in town savvies the only actual Frenchman in Rapid is that Alexandre. The cook's Chinese. Don't let on I said, but most French cooks on the West Coast is Chinese. They got a *cuisine,* too, the Chinese do, so their chefs got the touch, and I guess the only thing real different is all the cream and butter the French put in everything, which Merry Lee tells me gives her and most of her countrymen indigestion.

Our table was tucked into a window nook and half-screened by the heavy red velvet curtains so we would have to try real hard to scare the horses—or the other patrons for that matter—and it overlooked the gorge and the river. The oldest mill in town—the one where they sawed the lumber that built this hotel we're in, and the lumber for the Hôtel Ma Cherie as well—is downstream from the Riverside, which sits up above the rapids that give the city its moniker. So when Priya and me turned our heads, we looked down at the smoky twilit water fuming and roiling phosphorescent white under electric arc lamps, like it was picked out in radium paint. And beyond that, the mill and its electric lights, flooding up the waterwheel as it turned all slow and majestic down below. It was February, and there was a bit of ice, but it don't freeze up hard in Rapid City the way it does back in Hay Camp where I grew up before Da died. Still, Priya found the whole thing fascinating. And it was cold enough for her: she came from a place so tropic I can't even rightly imagine it (I know this because every time she talks about it I find out I've been imagining some bit of it wrong) and she couldn't ever seem to get warm enough.

We was so busy staring at that waterwheel, I'm embarrassed to say, we forgot to even look at the menus before the waiter came around and asked us what we'd like to drink. I hemmed a bit; Priya, who is cool as a long dip in that river down there, said, "A bottle of champagne, please." She cocked her eyebrows at me, her face all gilded up with candlelight. "It goes with everything."

I laughed so hard I had to smother it in my water glass to stop from being a scene. It was a deadpan imitation of

Miss Bethel, one of the ladies back at the Cherry Hotel, and since Miss Bethel was about the classiest mab who ever worked on her back, it got that biscuit shooter's attention. He bobbed his head and took off.

I was glad to see Priya perk up a little. She'd been stewing all day about her da's latest letter, which apparently hadn't been no picnic, and I was probably glad I couldn't read Tamil. Not that I could have read it anyway, because Priya had gotten up before sunrise this morning, walked into the kitchen, and burned it. Her da wanted her to come home and get married off, and he weren't being nice about it, either.

Before the waiter even came back a young Negro boy showed up with a basket of butter and bread so fresh the steam was still rising from it.

Well, maybe not that fresh. It didn't look cut hot—bread kind of squishes down when you do that, which I learned from somebody I still miss about every time I eat a biscuit—but cooled, cut, and reheated. Hotels, like whores, got all kind of little tricks they don't tell you too many details on, make you think you're getting something special.

It sure tasted good, though. It was early enough in the year that the butter was white, because the cows was eating silage, but I was just as glad they hadn't colored the cream yellow when they churned it. They use carrot juice to do the color, and the butter never tastes right to me after. My ma was Danish—she's the one named me Karen, before she died—and she was real particular about her butter.

The waiter came back with a bottle. Since Priya was wearing an evening coat and a necktie, he clearly decided that she was the boss. He showed her the bottle—a little dusty, still cool from the depths of the vaulted stone wine cellar that served as a bragging point for the Riverside's management—and while I was buttering my second piece of bread he untwisted the cage and eased the cork out into a clean white towel. I wonder if he knew why I looked down and smiled. Miss Bethel would have been proud of his professionalism.

When he pulled the towel away, a beautiful curl of pure white vapor rose up from the neck of the bottle as if from the water breaking on the rocks below, and I sighed. Then he gave me a little wink and a smile, produced two shallow glasses like it was legerdemain, and poured first for Priya and then, when she nodded over it, for me. He left the bottle in a bucket of ice beside the table, and by then I'd figured out what I wanted and we ordered—or Priya ordered for me, because that's how the waiter decided we was doing things.

It was all pretty fine. I don't mind being treated like a lady. Especially when Priya's the one doing the treating.

People back east got this idea we're all barbarians out in the settlement, but I wager they don't get oysters like ours back in New York. Well, maybe they do; I guess it's got a harbor.

Anyway, with all that outside to feast our eyes on and all that anticipated good food to whet our appetites after, and the anticipation of going home to our own little house, it took something indeed to direct our attention back inside.

But then those two girls came in and was seated at the table next to us, and they was dressed up like Easter, the both of 'em, with one in emerald watered silk and the other in indigo. They rustled as they moved, and their shady wide-brim hats were cocked at exactly the same angle. The lace was white at their cuffs and fell heavy across the backs of their hands. One was tall and one was short; they both was buxom with a little nipped-in waist and a good curve on 'em under the bustle. They both was fair, and each one had hair hennaed auburn-purple and dressed in curls. The short one was wearing a lace coat over her dress that I'm not ashamed to say I envied a little. The tall one had given her wrap to the maître d'.

They pulled some of the hairier eyeballs off Priya and me, and I'd be lying if I said I weren't grateful. They knew just how to work the attention. When they faced each other across the two-top, those hats framed them so they looked just like a papercut. That's a practiced skill, like an actor's stagecraft, and there's a lot of folk don't know it. Every eye in the room was on 'em: you don't see too many unaccompanied ladies out in a frontier town, unless they're doing the marketing of a morning, or unless they don't care to be accompanied.

I had to respect that. I had to respect that, and the white kid gloves, and all the work that went into getting their hair to fall just so. Professional respect, though I wasn't in the trade anymore. Though who knows. Maybe they was respectable ladies and cutting a figure just for the fun of it, and not as good advertising to drum up clientele.

They might have been sisters or they might have been a sister act. Their profiles weren't too similar—the little one had a good strong nose with a warmblood's Roman bump in it, and the tall one had a button nose like a Shetland pony—but they was working the angle all right. The tall one had a narrower face, while the little one had lips like couch cushions you just wanted to lay yourself down on. If I hadn't been sitting next to my own glorious Priya, I might have been thinking of doing just that.

There was one other woman dining alone in the hotel that night, and getting attention from the miners and such—but she was gray haired and soft chinned, with a widowed air of independence and a little pinned hat, and I suspected from the likeness on the bills posted outside that she might actually be the lady performer we were planning on ending the night with. She glanced over at the girls once, arched her brows, and went back to her tea like it was no concern of hers—but a funny expression passed her face for just a second before she smoothed it. I probably wouldn't have noticed none, except I used to make my living noticing little expressions and tells and you never quite get out of the habit.

In any case, I kept an eye on those girls. The men, for all they want us around when they want us around, sure don't want us around the minute we turn inconvenient. So we girls look out for one another. There ain't no such thing as men's work in a parlor house. And I was still a paid-up dues-current member of the Ancient and Honorable Guild of Seamstresses and would be until the day I died, even if I was a lady rancher and horsebreaker now by profession and didn't pay no sewing machine tax no more.

So anyway, to bring us back to the present moment, maybe I'm an old jade at seventeen. But I also had an illusionist for a john once upon a time and he told me a few things that rapidly disappointed my early interest in Spiritualism, which I suppose was a natural sort of thing for a young orphan to yearn after.

So when we was getting to the end of our dinner and the table started thumping, I guessed I knowed what was what, and I didn't pay it no nevermind. Priya, who's got some damned good reasons to be high-strung, jumped in her seat and looked ready to bolt. I put my hand on her knee under the table and she settled, and seemed to settle more when I picked up my fork unconcernedly and applied it to the edge of my peach tart.

I admit, I was motivated at that point more by dessert than by curiosity. And if those girls were working on getting out of a tab, well, I had money in my pocket and didn't mind paying, and I wanted to see the show, and furthermore I had hopes of being welcome back in the Rain City Riverside sometime.

Why take a risk when you ain't got to?

———————

The place has a bloody enough reputation to support a haint or three. So the haunting might even be true, especially if my illusionist beau didn't turn out to know everything, as you might not be surprised to know men once in a while don't. On the other hand, I've lived in Rapid City long enough to know ain't nobody ever seen a ghost in the hotel, or if they has done, management's got 'em paid off handsome enough to keep it to themselves. There's plenty of folks as say they've heard one, but there's plenty of folks who will make a sure-thing ghost out of a couple of foundation creaks and a cat jumping off a bookshelf in the middle of the night.

I'd say "sure as shootin'," but as somebody who's been pretty well shot at, you know the thing is shooting just ain't that sure.

Anyway, whether it was a haunting or a confidence job, we was having a harder and harder time concentrating on the food with all that rattling and banging, and other parties around the place was taking notice, too.

The old woman—in her widow's weeds just like she was back in New York City—she weren't fazed none and didn't look up from her cup of tea, though I saw her eyes slide sideways once. Her face under the little black pill cap was kind and velvety, the way some older women's faces get, and her expression never shifted. One fellow—a colored man I thought was probably a traveling businessman of some sort because he was wearing a bottle green suit and eating alone—signed his check quick and made for the inside entrance that led deeper into the hotel. A couple, locals I thought, man and woman out for a nice dinner, had been respectively dawdling over soup, eating daintily with a napkin in hand (her) and trenchering through a tray of oysters (him). *They* both quit their work and stared.

The biggest and rowdiest party had been three Yukon miners fresh back in civilization. You could spot 'em by their pink cheeks where the beards had been scraped off—on the two white ones anyway—and the fingernails still black with ground-in dirt despite the sea voyage and the hot baths they must have bought before they slipped on their new ready-made suits. One of 'em was still wearing his down-at-the-heel boots, but they'd obviously done pretty well in the goldfields. Most of the other kind don't come back at all. Either they die up there, or they stay in Anchorage and take up with the fishery or they sell stuff to the next crop of would-be millionaires at six or seven markups. They barely looked over at the ruckus the girls was causing—or barely more than they had been, since they'd been staring a bit to begin with, and possibly trying to impress the girls with their loud talk about sled dog disasters and borglums.

I may have been eavesdropping on the borglum talk a little, too, if you can call it eavesdropping when the speaker aims to be overheard. I ain't from no mining town originally, and Rapid ain't so much a mining town as a way station—but ain't almost nobody talk like miners, and rumors get around. The borglums, so they call 'em—the little people as live in mines—they're supposed to be pretty friendly mostly. They knock and warn about poison gas and mine cave-ins and such. But you can make 'em angry, or so these lot were claiming.

Priya, as if noticing my attention had wandered, said, "Do you think those young women are planning to four-flush the restaurant?"

Priya's diction is so perfect; her accent—except the little musicality that I guess comes from growing up speaking Hindi or Tamil or whatever—is so English and precise that it never fails to make me giggle when she spouts some bit of terrible local color she's picked up from living around me.

I said, "Well, unless all them gems is paste, they've got some money on 'em. But I know some chiselers make it a point of pride never to pay an honest sum even if they have it. I'd go ahead and finish your dessert."

Priya poked the tart with her fork and lifted her eyebrows suggestively and I had to push my own finger against my knife point to keep from braying with laughter in the most undignified manner.

We settled back down and set in with our forks to lay a serious siege on that peach tart. We hadn't hardly got four more bites in, though, when the rattling silverware and rocking top switched to a big, heavy, hollow knocking like somebody banging on a log drum, like some of the Indians use. Our own American Indians, I mean, not Priya's kind.

_____

The girls still sat on either side of the table, eyes wide and arms by their sides, seemingly frozen in their places. The candles in their silver sticks guttered. The restaurant's expensive Chinese carpets were not as nice as the one Priya's ma had shipped us all the way from India for our new house, and—I would bet a good filly colt—with Priya's da, who didn't approve of us none, none the wiser. But between the carpets and the legs of the girls' two-top, a gap of some eight inches had developed and was rapidly widening to near a foot.

Now it so happens that regular john I used to have, the one who was a stage magician—an illusionist, they call themselves—had a side job as a medium, cheating Spiritualists when the stage bookings was slow. Well, you might know this already, but it just so happens men will tell you just about anything at all when they're relaxed enough, no matter if it's a professional secret or a personal one. You just got to catch 'em in the right mood, if you take my meaning. Also, ten times out of ten men who pay for all night is paying for it to impress other men with their virility. Maybe one in a hundred will really make you lose much sleep. And for the rest, talk is as pleasant a way as any to pass the time.

This trick was one of the ones who was really more

paying for somebody to listen to him tell his life story than somebody to roger blue in both sets of cheeks. But he made a fine living as a Spiritualist, if a shabby one as a prestidigitator, and since he was paying me for my time and the talk was interesting, I didn't mind at all. He told me that the way they lifted the tables like that—levitated, he called it—with their hands on top and their feet in plain sight on the floor, was one of two ways. Either they used fake feet and shoes, visible under the edge of the tablecloth or their skirts and flounces, or they used extensible poles that they wedged with their legs, and balanced the tables on that. His take was that most Spiritualists was dishonest illusionists, though some were right fine ones.

He probably saw my face fall when he told me all about the tricks they use, though—because he also told me that he didn't know but some of 'em was on the up-and-up, or at least thought they was. It griped him that he could make more money pretending to work real magic than amazing people with his illusions, but the way he saw it, well, most people want to be fooled and will pay you to do it, especially if you make them feel good about themselves along the way.

I see it a little differently. Men own almost all of everything in the world, and white men moreover, and they don't scruple how they get it. If the rest of us have to engage in a little trickery now and again to get by, well, if they didn't want us to cheat they should have made the rules fair in the first place.

Not that I judge, though there's plenty as would judge me. There's a lot of make-believe in the profession I used to follow, don't get me wrong. And I don't know too much about most people, but I know a lot about the men who come to parlor houses. They sure do want an illusion, about you and about themselves. But it seems to me, and maybe it's not surprising, that a lot of wives and lady friends provide that same illusion, and they don't get Sundays off and they got to clean as well.

It's funny, ain't it, that nobody holds giving men the illusion they want about themselves against wives, though they hold it against the Sisters. And nobody holds it against illusionists, though they do against Spiritualists. I'm not quite sure how to explain what I'm driving at, except it seems to me that these things is all linked.

Especially as most of them Spiritualists is women. Near as I can tell the only three ways for a lady illusionist to make a living is by pretending to be a medium operating under the control of a spirit guide, pretending to be a lovely assistant, or doing what Mrs. Horner is doing and performing as her husband's relict.

I guess everything a woman does is more respectable if the world can see that she's owned by some man as can take credit for it.

Anyway, I tapped Priya's hand and pointed just a little without lifting my fingers away from the table. She turned—I figured it was okay now, since the sister act was so manifestly looking for attention—and gawped when she eyeballed what was going on. She clamped her mouth shut, lips in a thin line for a second before she snorted and said, "Sleight of hand."

"Sleight of knee, more like."

"What do you think the flash lay is?"

"It's a long way to go for a free lunch."

Everybody seemed plumb frozen in place. A stream of coffee was dribbling from that silver pot's spout as it sagged in the hand of the busboy, whose fingers was nevertheless paled at the knuckles from clutching it. The drunken gold miners had even simmered down and was just staring.

And then the most surprising thing of all happened. The lady in the widow's weeds, the one with the velvety face, folded her napkin in precise and irritated folds, laid it down beside her plate, and stood her up and turned her about and marched over to the sister act and said, in a clear grandmother voice, "Miss Arcade, I never knew you had a sister."

And you know, that woman *was* old enough to be their grandmother, and those rude girls did not even look up at her. The name, though—Arcade—that tickled a bell. There was, indeed, a pretty well-known pair of Spiritualists who went by that handle.

I was distracted from thinking about that because the little one started speaking in tongues, and it weren't no easy thing to listen to. It weren't so much like what I heard in this revival tent one time when I was a little girl (Da hustled me out of there, he told Ma later, "before the snake handling could begin"), which had been all chanted sounds and babble. This was more like that hyperbole such as is printed down the side of a patent-medicine soft-soap label that you read to entertain yourself while you're washing your hair.

It'd been such a real nice supper, too. Stayed real nice even through the table levitation.

Stayed real nice right up until *our* table decided to join in the fun. After five shatteringly loud knocks I would have sworn I felt up through my silverware, it hopped into the air and flipped over, seemingly all by its lonesome. It landed with a crash of crockery and spilled my peach tart with brandied cream all over my girlfriend's good new trousers. I was pretty put out about that, despite it being made with canned fruit, seeing as how I hadn't gotten around more than a quarter of it because I was taking tiny, proper lady bites that would have made Miss Francina proud of my table manners.

What I should have done is, I should have dropped money on what was left of the table, grabbed Priya's hand, and walked out of that hotel dining room and kept on walking. But I had just about managed to get Priya to cheer up and really smile and I didn't want to give that up. And—I got to admit it—I was curious as a damned cat. And I was a little taken aback that our table had gotten into the action, because I'd thought I had the situation figured and that was some kind of contrary evidence right there.

That's what I should have done. What I *did* do was, I flinched back against the wall beside the window, which I had my back to, as was proper for a lady, and I wound up half-tangled in those expensive curtains. So there weren't nothing I could do about it when Priya leaped out of her chair and sent it over with a second crash. She spun around on her toe to confront the noise, her fists up to fight, and I saw the moment in the set of her shoulders when that whirl of self-defense turned into shame.

She held her hand up to cover her face, embarrassed by how she'd started, but nobody in the restaurant except me was looking at her. They wasn't even looking at our spilled dessert. Because, as I found out following their gazes, they was all looking at the confrontation between the woman who made me miss a grandmother I'd never met and the two young ladies I was coming to unexpectedly admire. The old woman was standing over them, waving a bottle of something under the little one's nose. Smelling salts, and if she weren't really in a trance I admired her self-control, because those things stink something awful.

I couldn't figure how they'd managed to flip *my* table. They hadn't walked anywhere close enough to get a line around one of the legs. The best I could come up with was that maybe the busboy was in cahoots, but I didn't have no evidence of that, you understand. It was just a speculation that fitted the evidence, as my friend Marshal Reeves would have said.

Alexandre the maître d' was moving over to break up the altercation as smooth as if he were on caster wheels, but I noticed that the waiter had vanished. That might have been suspicious, and I was finding it so when I got distracted by another act in the play.

The short girl was still babbling, and the tall one was gripping the arms of her chair, crowded back into the caning like a snake was reared up before her. Her eyes was wide and her hair had slipped into disarray, and she was staring at her sister with what looked like genuine shock and fear.

The grandmotherly woman sighed, marched back over to her own table as the nearest one that weren't overturned nor levitating, picked up a goblet with water in it cold enough to frost the cut glass, marched back in a sweep of black organza, and dashed the contents right into the face of the shorter girl.

The girl stopped short, spluttering. Her eyes flew open. It looked like some of the water had gone up her nose, and that ain't pleasant nohow.

The table came crashing down, and by some wonder nothing on it spilled—possibly because most of it was et up already—though some white wine slopped out onto the tablecloth. The shorter girl's hands flew to her collarbones and her charmingly exposed décolletage, and she gasped, "My silk dress!"

"Don't you worry your head about it. A little steam and a white cotton handkerchief and those water spots will come right out. Your maid can do it for you, Miss Arcade. I'm sure that she knows how." The grandmotherly lady spoke kindly, but you could tell from the crinkle in her velvety cheek that she didn't think the young woman had a maid to sort her wardrobe for her.

At that moment, the waiter came back in with Constable Waterson, and I felt right sorry for having come over all suspicious of him. The waiter, I mean. Not Constable Waterson, who was an all right sort of a lawman for a stick-in-the-mud. He arrived as the young ladies was standing up and fussing their skirts and possibly hiding some paraphernalia in there.

"All right, then," the constable said to the maître d'. "Set me straight."

"These young ladies," Alexandre said in his furry-sounding accent, "are causing a disturbance, as you can see. The hotel should like them removed from the premises."

"A disturbance!" said the taller one. Her face was a study in wounded innocence. She had big eyes without too much kohl around them, and she widened them convincingly. "That's likely! There was a disturbance indeed, in that our supper table assaulted us, and this creature assaulted my sister."

"Her *sister*," said the widow, "used to work for my husband. And me."

The tall girl talked right over her. "But it was none of our doing. We have done absolutely nothing to deserve this . . . bum's rush. If anything, this woman should be paying to replace my sister's gown, which is ruined."

"I see," said the constable. "I suppose you don't think you should be paying for your dinner, either?"

The smaller one said, with dignity, "Would you?"

Waterson sighed and pulled out his notebook. He had a pencil stub and a put-upon expression and appeared ready to make a night of it if he had to. "Names, ladies?"

"I'm Miss Hypatia Arcade," the smaller and older one said. "This is my sister, Hilaria."

Some parents do cruel things to their children, and ain't no mistake, but something about the ring of pride in her voice as she said it made me wonder if it was the older generation that had inflicted that particular unlikelihood or if they had selected it for themselves. It ain't on me to judge, though, and I once knew a fellow rejoiced in the moniker of Tribulation Goodenough. Came by it honestly, too, though I suspect Captain Minneapolis Colony got a little help along the way.

"And I'm Mrs. Micajah Horner," the velvet-faced woman said. A little thrill went through me as she pronounced her name. "And I contend these two are mountebanks, and ought to be ashamed of themselves."

She probably knew a mountebank when she saw one, too. I recognized that name. Her husband's name, I mean, and not the missus part. It was the magician's widow. Priya and me was here tonight in part because I'd been obsessed with her late husband ever since I was a little girl. I saw his red and yellow traveling posters when Da took me into the city to trade horses. I'd read newspaper accounts and magazine descriptions of his performances and I'd pined after the chance to see him myself someday. When I'd read he'd died, I'd felt a real grief.

He was famous—honest famous, like Sarah Bernhardt or Mark Twain or Wild Bill—too, and not just possessed of some local notoriety. There was a huge fuss when he died: it was a fortnight scandal, and all the papers said he and his widow had set up a special password by which he could prove it was really him talking if he contacted her from beyond the grave. His widow was demonstrating a number of her dead husband's illusions at the opera house next door tonight, the Riverside's auditorium being too small for the crowd expected. Priya'd got tickets as her moving-in-together gift to me.

Priya had sorted herself all right. I came around the table and put my shoulder next to hers like we was in harness. I could tell she was itching to squeeze my hand, and if we'd just been friends I would have grabbed hers in a heartbeat. But we had to observe the proprieties in public, seeing as how we was illegal and immoral and probably fattening, too, and even if the mayor was a friend of ours we were as subject to the full weight and fury of the law just for existing as these two young ladies was for scamming.

If they was scamming. I shot a sideways look back at our flipped table. I still couldn't figure out how they might have managed that. I wondered if Mrs. Horner had a theory. She was frowning at the mess like she just might.

Those girls had drawn a crowd. The couple stayed at their table, heads bent together, stealing occasional glances sideways at the fun. But the little gang of fresh-scrubbed returning miners, well, they got right up and gathered round, helping to quiet matters just as enormously as you might expect.

"My husband," said Mrs. Horner, who had an upright patrician posture that I might have found damned intimidating if Miss Bethel hadn't taught me the trick of it herself, "was an illusionist. He devoted his life to entertaining people, and to debunking Spiritualist nonsense, and I tell you right now that there are any number of ways to create the illusion that a table is levitating itself."

"That girl was talking like a snake handler," one of the miners put in helpfully, pointing at Hypatia. She ignored him regally, flipping her lace coat into more attractive folds.

Waterson was wavering. I could tell by the way he was frowning at his pencil.

Waterson's not a bad policeman, nor even a bad man, as such things go. But he ain't real creative, and he could probably be more assertive. Which to be honest usually suits me just fine. If it had just been the bum's rush I might have stood back. But I suspected that if I let Mrs. Horner keep working on them, Waterson would be fixing to arrest the Misses Arcade, and I hated to see a couple of Sisters get fitted for iron bracelets.

"Excuse me, Constable," I said, in my spunnest-sugar

voice. "You might remember me. We met at the old Hôtel Mon Cherie before it burnt down. My name is Miss Karen Memery, but back then they called me Prairie Dove." It was my old house name, and I saw him blanch a little as he recognized me. No honest cop likes polite society to pick up a hint he might be accepting favors on the side. I'd guess the dishonest ones like it even less.

I had his attention anyway, and as his frown deepened I stepped aside and moved it on to the overturned table and to the sad remains of the coffee and peach tart. "My table overturned, too, and I will testify that the Misses Arcade were nowhere nearby when it happened."

"Miss Memery," the maître d' said hastily. "Of course we will not charge you or Miss Swati for your food—"

"Not at all," I said. "Of course we're paying." I looked over at the mess. "Though if you could manage to wrap up a couple of tarts to go, that would be a treasure."

Well, we was all quiet for a moment, and then Hilaria nodded definitively, as if that proved some point she had been making. Hypatia's gaze met mine, and there was a challenge in it.

"I'll consent to be searched for any table-levitating gadgets," said Hypatia. "But only by a lady. It would be improper otherwise."

"Well," said Mrs. Horner. "I'm a lady."

"I don't want to her to touch me," Hypatia said, dabbing at a wet spot on her dress. "I don't trust her not to plant something."

I bet Mr. Horner had enjoyed being caught between *these* two.

I smiled. "I'm a lady also."

———————

Well, two seconds after I said that, as soon as the attention was off us, Priya caught my elbow hard. I don't think she meant it to hurt, but she's got a grip on her, and mechanic's calluses, and her emotions was running high. Her expression was smooth, with all her practice of showing nothing of what she felt. What she bent toward me to whisper was, "I don't want us getting close to those girls. I would feel safer if you kept your distance from them."

Well, of course at first I thought, how dare she tell me who to spend my time with. But then I thought she's got a right, too, to decide who she wants to associate with.

I kissed her on the cheek, a sisterly peck I thought I could get away with in public, especially if I did it bold as brass in front of everybody as if it weren't nothing. "You got a specific problem with them?"

She shrugged. Her downcast dark eyes seemed

opaque in that light. "I would just feel safer if you kept your distance."

———————

Me and Mrs. Horner and them erstwhile redheads went into the cloakroom with Constable Waterson standing outside, listening through the drape over the doorway, and Mrs. Horner stood back and watched while I ran my hands over both the Arcade sisters in turn. I had learned how to do a thorough frisk at the parlor house, and I expected to find rods and whatnot under their skirts, and maybe be offered money to keep quiet, but there weren't nothing under there but the usual bits you'd expect. Hypatia wisely had a little derringer in her décolletage—a bosom gun for a bosom that matched up with the rest of her, which was to say she had a figure of consequence. Hilaria had a set of knuckle-dusters in a garter on a thoroughbred leg, and that seemed sensible, too. I managed not to linger running my hands over Hypatia, which was an act of will, and something I wish more men would manage. I understand how it feels to touch something pleasant, believe you me, and it's right hard to stop stroking a kitten—but even if you're feeling something inside, you got no call to make it somebody else's problem less'n you know it's welcome trouble.

They caught my eye over the weapons, and I shrugged and showed 'em mine. Mrs. Horner watched with pursed lips but didn't say boo.

We hadn't discussed nothing: there was nothing we could discuss, with Waterson standing right by the door. But in a world where men walk around with guns on their hips and their saddles, I don't see anything unusual about a woman wishing to protect herself. And it ain't socially acceptable for us to strap an iron on our hip, so either we can be eccentrics like Calamity Jane or we can slide a little insurance into an inconspicuous spot.

I did notice that maybe the boning in their corsets was a little heavy for such slim young things, and there was a spot across the tummy of each one that had a kind of joint, which ain't something that's a regular feature of undergarments in my experience, but nothing I could have pointed to and said there was funny business. Mrs. Horner didn't give up looking suspicious, but she looked curious, too, and I was starting to figure she had one of those minds that couldn't let go a problem. Also, I'd reckoned out by then that she knew at least one of these two pretty darn well, and I didn't get where I am today by keeping a checkrein on my curiosity.

Hypatia, once I smoothed her ruffles down and stepped back, laid her lashes across her cheeks and looked through them at me and said, without any at-

Elizabeth Bear

tempt to muffle her tones, "You've lost somebody dear to you, haven't you, Miss Memery?"

Well, that weren't no great stretch. Pretty near everybody has. It's a rough old world for staying alive in. But she was a kind of pretty that went right down my spine, and I felt a little unworthy thrill as she licked that pouting lower lip and smiled at me. I've worked enough men to know how it goes, and I knowed I was being worked. And I love Priya with all my heart, don't get me wrong.

But there's only ever been Priya, and before her Belle, the girl who found me at the train station and gave me a bed for one night when I first got to Rapid City. She brought me to Madame Damnable's in the morning, and I never knew her last name or even her real first name, and I know for a fact that she got a finder's fee for me. But she did me a kindness bringing me to Madame, and she didn't lie to me about what kind of an establishment it was and let me make my own decision—and she also figured out what kind of a girl I was before I knew myself.

"It's all right to sell your blood to some man," she'd told me, "but it'd be a damned shame to actually sell one your virginity. They don't want it because it's anything special to you; they just want to collect it so nobody else can't have it, and you shouldn't go through life thinking that's all there is."

And she'd shown me a thing or two I'd had cause to be grateful for since.

44

So I weren't naive. I knowed Hypatia was running me. That didn't stop it being effective, though. Especially when she said, "There's a whisper about you. Someone hovers over you, a protective spirit. Her hair is bright, though—not dark, like yours."

Reader, it went through my heart like a cake-testing wire, narrow and perfectly sharp. Mrs. Horner muttered something disgusted. I found myself looking down into eyes as clear and bright as polished water.

"She has a message for you," Hypatia said. "And there's someone with a message for your friend as well."

I wanted to believe so bad I had to step back away from her. My mouth filled up with that hollow watery taste, and my gut went hollow, too, and just as watery.

"We'll talk later," I said. "If you really have a message."

"And your friend?" Hilaria put in protectively. "She doesn't like us."

I didn't even see the signal pass between them. If there was a signal. It could have just been honest sisterly guardianship. And I wanted so bad to believe that somehow, *somehow*, Ma could speak to me through this petite, pretty little package.

She'll come around, I thought. But what I said was, "You better tidy your garments. I'm gonna go call in the man."

So I fetched Waterson in, once Hypatia and Hilaria

had resettled themselves. Priya came with him: she'd been waiting by the door, too, and just seeing her warmed me, even if her face was drawn up under the cheekbones and pinched around the mouth in tiny lines. I gave her a tiny smile and turned to Waterson and said just that to him. "I ain't found no funny business."

He nodded. "Ladies," he said formally to the Arcade sisters, "the hotel has agreed to settle your bill, as long as there aren't any more disturbances."

The sisters looked at each other while I walked over to stand next to Priya. My love crops her hair down like a woman who's had a fever, so it won't get caught up in gears and such. It was just an inch or two long, and it revealed all the delicate lines of her jaw and throat and cheeks and the bones of her skull, and she was so beautiful it stuck my throat closed. I thought I might die from not being able to reach out and touch her, but she smiled at me and the clamps around my heart eased open just a little and I could get a whole deep breath.

"And what do they want in return?" Hypatia asked skeptically.

"The hotel manager asked you to sign this form," Waterson said. He held it out. "It absolves the hotel of any responsibility for any injury or harm you might come to."

Hilaria cocked her head skeptically at Mrs. Horner. "And what about this old lady with the water glass?"

"If you avoid me, I'll agree to avoid you."

They traded a stare, but after a bit Hilaria nodded.

Waterson said, "You're moving on in the morning."

It wasn't a question. Hypatia pursed her lips and looked at her sister. Whether they had any blood between 'em or not, they sure had the silent communication thing down. Priya and I shared a similar glance. I was thinking, *Mrs. Horner is going to think I'm in cahoots with these two.*

Priya . . . well, I weren't rightly sure what she was thinking. And it bothered me I couldn't tell.

The taller Arcade said, "We will be here until Monday afternoon. I can show you our train tickets, Constable."

Waterson sighed. But they hadn't done anything illegal, not that he had caught them at, and he was, as I said, a law-abiding copper.

"Stay out of Mrs. Horner's way," he advised, "and you'll stay out of mine."

The girls agreed meekly. Too meekly, if you're asking me. But by then I was wondering again if maybe they weren't mountebanks at all. It *was* possible that we'd all run afoul of the Rain City Riverside's supposed resident ghost.

. . . And it weren't like me at all to be having such a hard time making up my mind.

So about that story I got by way of the Professor and

his acquaintance. It goes that Old Boston, the owner of the Griswold Claim in Alaska, spent him a little too much time out in the frozen wilds. Maybe he got greedy. Maybe it's just that it's damn hard to walk away from a hole in the ground when you're still picking gold out of it, and oftentimes for quite a little while even after.

Anyway, by the time when he was ready to ship back to Rapid, Old Boston had gone a little weak in the head.

How one man managed the violent deaths of himself, three other miners, one bartender, and a saloon girl in the hotel bar—and the blinding of that piano player—nobody knows one way or the other, nor how he got a pickaxe into the room or what happened to it afterward. Though I heard he'd brought his ironbound trunk with him—wouldn't be parted from it—and the trunk was smashed to flinders afterward, like an elephant had sat on it.

The whole story's whopperjawed either way, if you ask me. It's not like such a story needs a lot of work to be scandalous enough to be interesting, given all those murders and then a suicide. And the *Rapid City Republican* said he left a note as read: "I just don't want to do this anymore."

That's one reason it's a mite challenging to argue with. I wondered what Priya thought about it all, though, and I wondered if she'd ever even heard about the murders or if she believed in haints.

I found out quick enough. As soon as she had a moment's privacy with me—in a drawing room hung with ivory velvet flocked wallpaper and green marble tables with those little cat feet—Priya caught me by the elbow, put her mouth close to my ear, and said, "I don't know what you're getting us into this time, Karen, but I wish you would have discussed it with me first. I told you I weren't comfortable with those two! I asked you to do one thing, and you went behind my back and did another."

I jerked back and looked her in the eye. She was frowning at me, dead serious, and Priya usually had a little bit of a sparkle. "It ain't like I had a lot of opportunity to consult."

She looked at me and sighed. "We shall discuss it once we are home." She smiled a little, and it got wicked. "Or possibly in the morning."

I took a deep breath and said, "I was thinking of us staying at the hotel tonight after all. After the show. Just to, you know. Sort of keep an eye on things."

She blinked at me. I'd stunned her dead, which didn't happen often.

"It'll be late after the show, and it's a ways home, you know—"

"I do not think that is perhaps the best idea."

Some horses take a firm hand on the rein. And some toss their heads up at the slightest pressure, and got to be negotiated with. I'm enough of that second kind that I forgot, for half a second, that Priya's not even a fractious filly. She's more like a mule: she's smart and she knows she's smart and you don't just got to negotiate; you got to convince her she understands the whyfors of what you're up to and how it's in her own best interests—and yours—before she'll sign on.

If I'd been thinking straight at all, I would have said something else but what I did. "I won't have anybody in Rapid thinking I'm a mountebank. I *need* to find out what is going on here. And I'm worried about those girls, Pree."

"Those 'girls,'" she said, "are as old as we are. Older." She shook her cropped dark head. "This wouldn't have anything to do with the one who was spinning you the line about your poor dead mother wanting a last chat, would it?"

I got my back up, and I knew she saw it happen. Because she wrinkled up her mouth and said, "I knew going into this partnership that you would be chasing down every varmint and bringing home every lamed critter in the county. But this isn't a broke-wing sparrow, Karen. It's a stinging wasp. And what's more, you're offering to stand me up on our wedding night."

I opened my mouth to protest. "I'm not standing you up—"

"I am *not* staying in this hotel tonight," she said, with finality. "It has tables overturning and those girls you're so worried over are running some kind of a flash lay you and I do not begin to understand. What was under their skirts?"

I glanced around us to make sure nobody was within sight to listen and all the doors was closed. Sullenly, I said, "The tall one's got a knuckle-duster in her garter."

"And what else?"

Technically, it wasn't under her skirt, but I knew chopping logic with my sweetheart was not going to buy me anything I wanted to invest in right now. So I told her about the derringer. Priya cocked her head in that listening way that means she's thinking harder and faster than I can ever keep up with. She didn't make no fuss at all about me putting my fingers down a strange girl's bosom, though. She just said, "No lifting poles? No tiny engines or mechanicals?"

I shook my head. "Not that I savvied."

"That surprises me."

"Surprised me, too," I admitted. "So everything I said to Waterson was the plain truth, if not the detailed version."

"I'm glad you did not lie to Waterson."

Maybe she unbent a little, and I breathed a sigh that the quarrel was ending. She'd stay with me, I was sure, once she knew I wasn't colluding. And she was right: it was our wedding night near enough. Plenty of new-hitched teams go away someplace for a day or two to get to know each other.

Then she said, "Now come home with me, Karen, please. You are my wife. I do not like it when you put yourself in danger, and you should not make decisions without consulting me."

What she'd said bounced once before it stuck, I think, and started to soak in. Because I stared at her, blinking, for at least a second or so before what she said made any bit of sense to me.

And then I didn't believe it. Sure, she wore the trousers in the family, except for when I was horsebreaking, but that was because she liked wearing trousers and I didn't, in particular. I remember thinking real clear and slow that if I had wanted that kind of treatment I could have married a man and had a lot less hassle. And then I felt myself get cold, which don't hardly happen, and I turned my shoulder to her and told her to suit herself and that I would be along home in the morning.

"Karen," she said.

I just shut her out. I didn't answer fast because I was biting my lip hard to keep from shouting at her.

"If that's the way you feel," I said finally, "you go on ahead. You ain't my husband and you ain't the boss of me, Priya darling. I got work to do here tonight, and I aim to do it."

She stared at me. I know 'cause I could see it out of the corner of my eye, though I wouldn't look at her straight. I was too het up, and anyway I was afraid if I did I might start crying.

I was sending Priya off to spend the first night in our own little house alone, and I felt terrible about it. I could tell by the way her neck straightened and her chin lifted up that she felt terrible about it, too. But she was coming over stubborn as is her way, and as for me I was so sore about that "wife" comment that I didn't even know what I was kicking at; I was just kicking.

Mad as I was, I hoped to hell it weren't an ill omen, us spending that night apart. I thought about asking her to stay for the show, at least, as we'd planned, and I expect if I had and she had we would have got over our mad and worked something out. But I didn't get it out fast enough. I guess my pride was in the way of my common sense, as happens sometimes, and they tripped over each other and both went down in a tangle.

Then she shrugged, and without another word she turned around, headed for the cloakroom, and left me standing there. And it happened that it didn't matter if I was looking at her square or not, because I just managed to hold that sob back until I heard the latch click, and not a greased second longer.

The ladies' parlor was on the way of being an antechamber to the powder room, which was fortuitous, because I weren't no sight to be seen in public. I ducked through the connecting door and found me a water closet to try and weep silently in. It's a hot mess crying in silk because you have to catch every tear and drop of snot before it touches the fabric, or the fabric will spot something terrible.

And so here's your big bad U.S. Deputy Marshal Karen Memery hunched on the lid of a fancy flush toilet in the nicest hotel north of San Fancy-cisco, holding her corset sides and trying not to sob out loud. One reason to learn to cry ladylike is that sobbing in a corset bruises up your rib cage something awful. Well, I ain't never had the knack of crying pretty, and that night weren't going to be the first time.

Nobody came in, and I finally wound down on my own. I took a deep breath, cautiously, and felt all the sore spots. I didn't just get the rib cage, but the diaphragm too, and that hurt enough that I managed to settle myself with it. I felt like a horse had kicked me right in the breadbasket, and I thought of my U.S. Marshal friend Bass Reeves, who was from Texas, teaching me about tortillas and how to grill a skirt steak, which was that same part of the animal, and slice it thin.

That was the bit on me that was hurting so bad. I wondered if I had tenderized it good.

That seemed to put a finish on the waterworks, so I hoisted myself out of the water closet, walked out to a sink, and washed my face in the cold tap water. The ranch didn't have no running water, just a well pump in the yard. Priya and I didn't mind—we could fetch and carry and boil, and knowing my Priya she'd be putting in some sort of Mad Science to run us piping-hot water for washing right into the kitchen before long—but I determined to enjoy the city luxury while I was here. I hadn't worn paint, not even rouge, because I was a respectable lady now, so my face didn't need repairs beyond the icy water to bring the swelling down.

I was dabbing myself dry on a hand towel white and fluffy enough that it could have served for the guests at Madame Damnable's, still careful not to spot my dress, when the door opened up and the velvet-faced lady in black stepped inside.

She didn't seem surprised to see me, from which I done surmised she'd seen two of us go in and only one come out, and that she knew there weren't no second entrance.

"Miz Horner," I said, in my politest, when she'd been staring at me a little while. Sizing me up, like.

"Well, young lady," Mrs. Horner said, "that constable informs me that you are an upstanding citizen, in your own way, and he says, I quote, 'She's the bravest girl in Rapid.' So I'm taking it upon myself, as a kindness, to say I hope you aren't wrapped up in any shenanigans with those henna-headed she-devils, and that if you are, you'll disentangle yourself fast as fast may be. They will do you no good in the long run. Immoral as cats, the pair of them, and as serving of themselves."

"Yes, ma'am," I said. Because whether her face was velvet or not, she weren't wearing it like it brooked no argument.

"You aren't in cahoots with those rampallions?"

"No, ma'am. I ain't never met them before tonight."

"'I haven't ever,'" she corrected, and for a moment she looked and sounded so much like an older version of Miss Bethel that I laughed out loud. It didn't do my bruised-up skirt steak no favors. I gasped and clutched my middle.

"God damn my fajitas," I said, right out loud, and had to stop myself from laughing again because that would have continued to hurt like the dickens.

Mrs. Horner studied my plumpness like she could see through the corset. "Young lady, you're not . . . expecting, are you?"

I almost laughed again but rescued myself in time. A good year of my life spent seamstressing without no needle, if you take my meaning, and I weren't about to turn up pregnant to Priya. Not unless she had talents that had remained hidden to me so far.

"No, ma'am," I said.

She cocked her head. You might say birdlike, if it were a bird big and tough enough that you'd be worried about it eating you if it took a decision to. "Maybe you can explain to me, then: Why do they call this hotel the Rain City Riverside when the city it's in is called Rapid?"

I knew all about that, and you may have noticed that I do like the sound of my own voice. "The Riverside is the oldest hotel in Rapid City. So the thing is Rapid City used to be named Rain City, which to tell you true I think is prettier, but the mayor back then and the city council decided 'Rain City' wasn't so great for tourism. And then they thought 'Rapid' sounded more like the sort of place people wanted to move to. So Rapid City it was. This would have been near on twenty, twenty-five years ago, long before I was born."

She got a little smirk like old folks do when you talk about your age, but I ignored it and kept talking. "Some folks held out, though, and one of them was old Mr. Bartholomew Roberts—no relation to the pirate as far as I know. He had already named his hotel the Rain City Riverside. You didn't get to be the third-richest man in the Washington Territory by paying to have perfectly good signs repainted."

"Not to mention," she remarked, "the elegant stonemasonry over the main entrance."

I nodded, my pin curls bobbing. "That's about the only place in the building you'll find any stonemasonry to speak of, though. The fireplaces and the foundations is laid stone, not dressed, and there ain't no dressed stone nor brick in the place anywhere."

"The whole foundation? Of this great place?"

"The Riverside is old enough that there weren't no dressed stone nor brick in Rapid at the time it was built and any suchlike had to be brought in from more civilized climes, so it's all laid stone and lumber, cut and planed from the first mill in town, before the Gold Rush even started. Which is the mill on the rapids you can see from the dining room, in point of fact. So it's woodframe, but they didn't spare no expense with what they had, if you take my meaning."

The place looks like it ought to be in San Francisco. It's a castle folly with the crenellations at the top, and in addition to that it's all over jigsaw gingerbread, and it's painted in the most amazing shades of violet, periwinkle, cream, lavender, and gray. It looks like something you ought to eat, not something you ought to go eat in, and it's got turrets and gables and balconies and foofaraws and a slated roof patterned in three different colors.

Sometimes I just like to stop and look at it.

She laughed, as if the question had been as much a test of my character as a request for information, and nodded judiciously. "If you're the bravest girl in Rapid City, then, I wonder. Would you like to earn some money?"

Whatever I had expected her to say, it weren't that. I contemplated it: Priya and me weren't destitute, not by a long shot, and the pretty little ranch was paid for. But I knowed pretty well how easy it was to get hurt gentling horses, and that was the only trade I had that Priya'd let me get away with plying anymore. Well, maybe real millinery.

The bills wouldn't stop coming if either of us had to stop working.

"Is it dangerous?"

"I rather think you'd find it intriguing," she said, which weren't exactly an answer. But then she continued, "No, not dangerous. Nor illegal. My sainted husband was an illusionist—"

I said, "I know. I've a ticket for your show tonight."

She smiled, and it seemed genuine. "Well, I was his

mechanical engineer. And some of the membership of the Pacific Coast Brotherhood of Illusionists will be attending the show tonight. Most of it I can handle on my own, but for one of his illusions it wouldn't hurt to have some help. Would you like to be my lovely assistant? It will be two hours of your time, including a little training."

"It don't involve burning no boxes of live doves or nothing? Because I won't be a party to none such as that."

"You do know a little."

I nodded.

"No animals harmed," she promised. "And I will pay you twenty dollars."

My eyes may have widened. Even in a Yukon Rush town, it was a fair chunk of change. Our fancy dinner hadn't cost more than a dollar for the both of us, and another fifty-cent piece for the champagne.

"That's a yes then. Good. Bring your lovely friend along," Mrs. Horner said with a smile.

"She'll just reverse-engineer your trick," I said, honestly, and then kicked myself. Priya would just about kill me for queering her chances. And then I thought that Priya would like to about kill me for other reasons right now anyway, and felt worse. Also, she'd be mad as hell to miss this, and I didn't know how to catch up with her with a message begging her to come back.

Well, served her right for walking out on me. Sure,

and I'd keep telling myself that to keep from thinking of her going home tonight to our little ranch house and climbing into our little tick bed all by herself. There's two reasons a feller does something stupid: one reason's pride and the other reason's love—or lust, at the least of it—and those reasons ain't no different for women. And when you got both tangled up in each other, well, that don't end well for nobody.

Mrs. Horner cocked her head at me, more like a curious tortoise with her lined face under her little ruched black hat than like a bird. "She's an engineer?"

"Just a tinkerer," I said. "She ain't got her Mad Science license yet. If she ever wants to get it, I mean." I half-hoped she would and half-hoped not. It was exciting to think of her doing all that inventing, but the backhouse was already going to be a mess, and I was scared to think of what she might do if she got the dueling bug or somewhat.

"You must bring her along then doubly," the old woman said firmly, and pressed two slips of paper into my hand. They had glossy printing on them. Passes, with the big word "BACKSTAGE." "It's *always* a pleasure to meet another engineer. Especially a woman."

I walked out of the ladies' room wondering if I could borrow or rent a horse to ride after Priya and bring her back for the show, or if it would be better to go to the Western Union office in the hotel lobby and ask the rider there to hustle after her with a telegram. Would she even come back for me? Thinking about asking left me curled up inside with worry about her refusing me again.

I weren't sure I could take it if I groveled and bribed and she told me a flat no.

But them two passes from Mrs. Horner felt like lead weights in my reticule. This wasn't something I could do without her, not and hope to ever make it up. I paused in the hall, and decided right then that I would in fact go talk to the concierge and get him to rent me a livery horse. My da was a horsebreaker before a wild colt killed him, and I can ride as good as anyone. I could catch her, all right, if anyone could—and at least try to get her to come back. And if she wouldn't, and if I missed out on Mrs. Horner's demonstration, well, I would have Priya, and in five years that would matter more than a magic show. Even a magic show I'd waited my whole life to see.

Priya *definitely* mattered more than my need to be up to my neck in whatever excitement was going on.

I had just about made up my mind when I remembered that I was still stinging from her trying to pull rank on me. If I was her wife and so I had to do what she said, then what did that make her to me? I had no intention of being no man's cur, no, nor no woman's neither. And if I went running after her and knuckled under, wouldn't that just prove that she could push me around any time she chose to?

Well, if these kinds of decisions was easy, nobody would ever make 'em wrong. This one had to be made fast, though, because she had a head start on me and that lead was opening out, so if I was going after her it had to happen now.

Pride's worth a lot; it's the only thing that can keep you walking when it feels like your feet's worn down to nubs. But as my ma would have said, you got to remember pride is a tool. You use it; you don't let it use you. And you don't sell your happiness 'cause your spine's too stiff to bend.

I took a deep breath. Once I had the livery pony I could always change my mind and come back, I supposed. If I didn't get a kind reception, and maybe an apology to match the one I probably should be offering her.

I squared my shoulders, and turned around—and nearly walked right into the Arcade sisters, who were two steps behind me, and the tall one was just clearing her throat as she reached out to tap my shoulder.

I drew up short, and they just about ripped their hems jumping back.

The smaller one—Hypatia—glanced over her shoulder, making sure the corridor was clear, while the tall one drew a breath. "Miss Memery?"

"Miss Arcade."

They looked at each other. Then Hypatia said, "Did you flip that table over?"

For somebody named Hilaria, the tall one sure did get her sister to do most of the talking.

Of all the things she could have said, that one brought me up the shortest. I'd been ready to shake them off and go take care of my home life, frankly, and as you can imagine given Priya's displeasure and the old lady's kindness, I weren't feeling none too sanguine about talking to the Arcade sisters after all. But I did it anyway, and I will admit right now as I could not admit to myself then that it was as much driven by curiosity as it was concern for their welfare.

Also, I'm not sure if they could have asked me anything that would have given me more of an unsettled feeling. And I have this bad habit when I'm uneasy: I got to get to the bottom of the question as quick as I possibly can.

I shook my head. "No, I did not. I take it you didn't, either, then? Which answers my question, actually," I said, real slow like. "I was trying to wrap my head around how you'd managed it while you was working the levitation trick with yours."

Their faces went white under the powder and paint. You could just watch the blood drain down to their toes, and the tall one put her hand out to steady herself against the small one's shoulder.

"I imagine Constable Waterson checked under your table," I continued. "And if he'd found anything, you'd be staying in a different and less comfortable establishment tonight for free. But all of that was a bit much for a bed and a dinner, so I have to wonder what else you're up to."

"You know," Hypatia said carefully, "we're Spiritualists. My control and my spirit guides are not always predictable."

"With your names you could hardly be otherwise," I allowed. They both looked at me sharply, but if there's one thing a retired whore can do, it's sound pleasant no matter what's coming out of her mouth—if she wants to. "Just your bad luck to run into Missus Horner while you was having a visitation, then. You know she and her late husband was skeptics, I assume?"

I slipped my fan out of my glove and used it gently to waft air across my face, though I had it in my mind it would be handy to rap a wrist with if one of 'em grabbed me. The end sticks is ebony and it's built solid—well, for a fan.

Now they was both looking at me not with speculation so much anymore as with cold calculation. I figured I had nothing to lose, and I still might learn something.

"I worked for her," Hypatia said. "Before I came to understand that my true calling was putting people in touch with their loved ones who have passed over, allowing them to make amends and pass along final messages." Her face smoothed into a saintly mask, which was an impressive trick under all that maquillage.

"So," I continued, "Missus Horner's your mark?"

"It's your mother, isn't it?" Hypatia asked, as if she hadn't heard me. "The lady with the bright hair. She was so young when she passed over. She was in so much pain. The pain is finished now, Karen. She just wants to tell you that she is at peace, and that she loves you and understands your choices, and that you will be together again one day."

I caught my breath in spite of myself. You tell yourself you know better. But she had such enormous, truthful eyes, soft and ingenuous as a blue-eyed Appaloosa's. You'd think I'd know enough about the kind of ponies as have eyes like that to have been on my guard, me of all people, but I was too busy falling into them.

They exchanged another look. Hilaria nodded, and Hypatia said, "You did intervene to prove our honesty, Miss Memery, and we know we owe you for the kindness. We're performing a séance this evening, and you'd be welcome to join us. We do not accept payment for our services."

Was Hilaria the business manager of the pair, then? No payment maybe, but I imagined they'd accept gifts, and their spirit guides probably demanded some sort of expensive tribute to show up to work.

I smiled and tried to pull myself together. It weren't too hard to figure out a girl like me might miss her mother. And there ain't no honor among grifters, not exactly, but there's a kind of camaraderie. It can take a lot of people to work a score. Sometimes, they set up shops—whole establishments where everybody who works there and most of the supposed clientele is in on the scam and draws a regular percentage for separating marks from their money. So they're used to working in crews.

Spiritualists are a little different, as they're usually singletons or pairs, and they do it all on their own. Some of 'em might even *believe* they've got a line to the other side.

Hell, there might be one or two out there that's the real machine. It galled me to think these girls might actually be what they was playing at. But that didn't stop me from wanting what they was selling, with all my heart and soul.

Ma. She weren't nothing but a little girl's memory to me. That she might know what I'd grown up as and still be proud . . . oh, I coveted that. And there was also the little fact that I couldn't explain my table flipping over as a wire or sleight of hand. And I would sell my own big toes and the tip of my nose if Priya had been in on it. Dishonesty wasn't in her, which was one reason she'd made a terrible prostitute.

Were the Arcade sisters just working my handle to pump out whether or not I'd twigged how their flash operated? Or was this little one and her line about bright-haired ghosts who loved me—just maybe—for real?

So I stood there and I thought about me and Priya's table flipping all on its lonesome, like that. I thought about my ma and da, and not getting to say good-bye to Da at all. Ma didn't die easy, but there was time to get used to the prospect that she was going on. Da just—the hand of God reached down and plucked him, and that was that. I thought about my friend Connie, who met a bad end in a way that was a little bit my fault, and how much I'd like to say I was sorry to her.

I wondered if apples mourned when one of their number quit the tree, to the hungry wind or a hungry hand. I bet not, or they'd taste like tears and not like sugar. It might be nice to be smooth and dumb as a fruit, and not to know what you was losing.

I knew what I'd lost. And I missed them so much it must have shown in my face, because Hilaria reached out in what looked exactly like human compassion and concern. She stroked my arm through my shawl.

It was probably playacting. It still made me choke up. I missed Ma and Da, sure. But I also missed Priya fiercely, especially when I thought about her fighting with her own da, and refusing to go back to India just because he was bossing her around. Was that the same as me feeling bossed around now? And if that was all she knew, wouldn't it behoove me to help her learn better, like a horse that's been broke badly?

We'd parted company in a fight and she'd gone out into the winter without me. How would I feel if something happened to her?

Just before Priya and me had gotten into the hire carriage that brought us here, we'd taken a last look around the little flat we'd been sharing since December. It was on the top floor of a wood-frame triple-decker that rattled when a big steam contrivance went by, and had an outdoor staircase steeper than some cliffsides. Now the flat was empty of every stick and scrap that hadn't come with the lease and there was nothing left to show that the second bedroom was just there for propriety. Well, it was Priya's work space, but other than that we just needed it so as the landlady could rent to us and claim she was ignorant of what went on up there if the law came calling.

We had been supposed to be going home to our own

place tonight. The house—a complete little ranch it was actually—that we'd bought for each other was an easy walk and an even easier ride from town. It was the best use either of us could think of for our reward money from the government on account of us being heroes that month.

We was lucky we lived in Washington Territory, where women could hold land in our own names. Even married women, which was something of a scandal some places back east, I'd heard. There was a time when I couldn't have brought my Priya into the Rain City Riverside, seeing as how she's Indian—Indian Indian, Tamil, not local Indian, and she wears trousers by preference—but the new mayor's made some changes in the town ordinances and it ain't legal none for them to deny us service now.

So it was me all by myself and my native Danish and Irish stubborn that had turned the night into a travesty. Well, to be honest, a touch of Priya's stubborn, too. But right this instant my indecision had melted away, and to go after her and fix things was all I wanted, and in her arms was the only place I wanted to be. We could work out the wife thing, and who was the boss of whom, in our own good time.

As long as we got that time. This was just a quarrel. Lovers have them. Surely this was just a quarrel. Not something we couldn't ever make up between the two of us.

One of us had to decide to make the gesture, was all. Reach out across the fight. And it was okay if it had to be me.

"Sorry, ladies," I said. "My friend and I have tickets to the magic show."

"Oh." Hilaria cocked her head, a meaningless, birdlike gesture—but a pretty one. I'd practiced it in front of mirrors myself. "It will be at midnight, afterward, when the spirit walls are thin. *We're* going to the magic show as well. But of course"—they exchanged glances—"your friend doesn't like us. It might suit your domestic harmony better if you stayed clear."

I bristled and made up my mind right then to go to her silly séance, which was what she had been planning all along, no doubt. "Oh, I'll square things with my friend, all right." But I couldn't resist getting a shot back in. "Do you think that's wise, going to the show, Missus Horner feeling like she does about you two?"

Hypatia dabbed her water-spotted gown. She said, with a small curve of her lush mouth, "We might as well get our money's worth," and laughed lightly.

It was a joke, of course, being as the hotel was covering their costs. My smile probably looked a little sickly on account of being all churned up inside about Priya getting further and further away, but at least I made the attempt to show I got it.

I swallowed hard to get my voice level and said, "Maybe I will. What room will you be in?"

"The Peacock Parlor," she said proudly. "It will be just a brief demonstration. For Constable Waterson and Missus Horner, among others, since the constable expressed a curiosity."

So Mrs. Horner was either taking the bait or painting them into a corner. Interesting.

"You ladies think that's wise, given the haint?"

"I have faith in the protection of my control," Hypatia said loftily, with a twinkle, and damned if I didn't still like her.

I thought about mentioning that the Peacock Parlor used to be the piano lounge, and was where those murders was supposed to have happened. She seemed pretty confident—either in her grift or in her gift—though, and it seemed mean to rattle her. So I said, "Maybe, then. The hotel laundry would probably steam that out for you, by the way. Especially if you tip well, and ask the ladies nicely."

She smiled at me and I smiled at her and Hilaria smiled at both of us. And I turned to make my way to the lobby and ask the concierge about a livery horse so I could go running after my beloved, no matter how wrongheaded and rockheaded she was being.

That was when the Rain City Riverside started to

rock on its foundations.

———————

You understand, the earth rattles out here every once in a while. It ain't like back at Hay Camp where we never felt a shake in my whole lifetime. We've got the volcanoes, and some sort of fault in the earth itself that jumps around, but it never does much harm. Still it's unsettling, and I was glad for the minute that the Riverside was a wood building and not mortar that might shake down on us.

But then I glanced out the window to judge the damage from a, you understand, outside perspective. And I realized that nothing else was shaking. Just the single building we was in.

That ain't natural.

———————

We looked at one another and without exchanging a word we ran for the lobby. All three of us, frilled skirts bouncing with their hoops, little heels clattering on the wood where it showed between the heavy Oriental carpets. I limp a little still—I got hurt in the fight last fall—and my knee and hip was killing me, but I kept up well enough to be out in front when we hit the landing at the top of the grand stairs in the front hall.

We skidded to a halt, clutching one another's arms for support. Down below us, the tall carved doors was shut up tight, and two bellhops was pushing at them without even shifting them in their frames. People surged in that lobby like the sea between the rocks, and going down there looked like the worst idea ever.

I looked over at Hypatia. "This your doing?"

Whiter than ever, she shook her head. And I knowed it was stupid to believe her, but I did.

"The spirits are in great confusion and disarray," Hilaria said.

I kept looking at Hypatia, because I'd figured out by now that when Hilaria did that she was trying to distract people from her "sister."

"It don't happen that you are a real medium, do it? 'Cause if you could spirit us up some advice on where to run toward to get out of this place, that would be a kindness."

Her pretty mouth went tight. "I am not in control of what the spirits reveal to me."

I thought about Ma and Da and I still wanted to believe. And then I felt sick for believing in spite of myself. You get invested in things—love affairs, politics, con games—and you tie yourself in knots trying to make reality match up to what would make you happiest. The mad part is, what would make you happiest is to get your cope on for what *is*, rather than what you would rather have happen.

So people follow their prophets, even when the prophets are wrong over and again. And that happens to the white man as often as the red, or any other.

All that piled through my head, but I didn't say a word of it. I just picked at my lip, which is a terrible habit, and muttered, "None of us ever is, sister."

The Riverside creaked on its foundations. I wondered if the chimneys would topple and come through the ceiling on all of us. The big crystal chandeliers was swaying and flickering something fierce, their fancy new electric lights casting drunken shadows over the nervous crowd milling about below, which didn't do nothing to settle 'em down to being less nervous. I thought of horses in a smoky barn and shuddered.

Maybe I was glad Priya'd walked out on me. At least she was safe.

Hilaria looked around wildly, a tendril of hair escaping her coif and adhering against her cheek, which was starting to shine through the makeup. "Is there anything we can do to get those people out of here?"

"Something's holding the door shut," I said.

Hypatia said, "What if we went through the kitchen?"

I thought of all those knives and boiling soup pots, and shuddered.

"Well," I said. "Looks like we got a real old-fashioned haint going on here."

"There's no such thing as a haunting."

I hadn't even heard Mrs. Horner come up on us, and here she was, speaking over Hypatia's shoulder in a voice that brooked no mischief. "My late husband and I investigated dozens of claims. Probably hundreds. Not one had a scrap of truth to it. But people want to believe."

People will argue stupid points at the damnedest times, and that, I am shamed to say, is exactly what I did. "What about jackalopes and catamounts? Hoop snakes? That lake monster they got in Scotland? I've seen a Sasquatch with my own eyes, you know."

Well, I'd got a glimpse of one. Close enough for argument.

"Those aren't ghosts. They're perfectly natural animals." She pushed past us and went to the wall. She was doing something with a part of the wall paneling. Trying to rip it off with a small pry bar she'd pulled from somewhere.

Did the magician's widow keep a pry bar in her reticule?

"Oh, so what's causing this, then?" Hypatia snapped. "Earthquake worms? A Cherufe?"

I didn't know what a Cherufe was, but I'd heard of earthquake worms. They was only supposed to be a South American thing, though, wasn't they?

Rapid City was a long way from Peru or even Mexico. The floor pitched under my feet while I was thinking about that. I hoped nobody was foolish enough to get in the lift. That's the first thing I heard from somebody when I came to Rapid City: you don't get in the lift when there's an earthquake.

That being the first day I'd come in from Hay Camp, I'd never experienced an earthquake *or* an elevator before, so it was more useful advice than you might think.

Mrs. Horner looked at me with irritation on her velvety face. "Won't you help me with this, Miss Memery? The riot bolt on those doors is thrown, and they won't come open unless it is retracted."

I felt a chill. A lot of the public buildings and fancier houses in our city, like in San Francisco, put in bolts to hold the doors shut in case there's rioting, again—anti-anybody, they claimed, but what they meant was anti-Chinese. Or, I suppose, in case the Russians come back and try their luck invading Rapid City again and we have got to defend it. Priya'd actually gotten work installing a few of them, since they have been so in demand this winter. They was usually triggered from a central location, like the manager's office or the desk, and they sealed up every door in the building.

Nobody would throw a riot bolt when the building was shaking like to fall down on all our heads, though.

I gathered up my skirts with a rustle and whooshed past the Arcades, who had bowed their heads together for a conference. Getting a little closer, I saw what she was working at. There was a little door, like a cabinet door, set flush into the wall and concealed behind a drapery and some gold cord. She had fitted the pry bar in next to the lock.

A steady stream of people was rushing down the grand staircase behind us, joining the crowd in the lobby. I didn't think that was the wisest thinking since Moses just right now, but there weren't much I could do to help them. So I helped Mrs. Horner instead, and we leaned on her pry bar with a will.

It didn't take much. The concealed cabinet was just supposed to be too hard for a hotel guest to open casually. It weren't a safe or nothing. It popped, splintering, and the Arcade sisters jumped and turned to us, eyes wide.

Mrs. Horner grinned a somewhat-toothy, somewhat-toothless, completely maniacal grin and handed me her pry bar. Inside the cabinet was a mess of levers and cables and electrical wires. I flinched when the old lady reached in there, but she had exactly the same expression of concentration as Priya got when she was mad-sciencing, so I just held the pry bar well away from the electrical stuff and stood back from it in my own person, too.

She did something with some switches. The terrible flickering light spun horribly as one of the swaying chandeliers started revolving on its cable. Some drapes around the lobby walls drew back, revealing damasked wallpaper and ranks of looking glasses, which rendered the effect that much more nauseating.

Mrs. Horner checked the effect over her shoulder and pursed her lips. "Not that," she decided.

I was glad to see we was in agreement.

Somebody downstairs screamed.

I was probably in agreement with that, also.

Then Mrs. Horner ejaculated, "Aha!" and grabbed a big lever off to one side in the compartment. She shoved it down confidently.

There was a big metal grinding sound, and the doors suddenly sagged on busted hinges. A couple of big men downstairs had the wherewithal to grab them and start wrestling them down. First one side and then the other got tossed out into the street, and a flood of people followed.

"Was it a short?" I asked Mrs. Horner.

She grabbed my hand on one side, and Hilaria's on the other, restraining us from following the crowd. "The lever wouldn't have worked if it was. Come on, girls—let the lobby clear out just a little, and once we've got a clear path to the door we'll go. We don't want to get trampled."

I was limping a bit by then on my bad hip, and what she said was just horse sense. She drew us to the side, out of line of sight, and I thought it was so nobody would come and fetch us. The hotel buckled and heaved around us. Hypatia had grabbed her sister's hand on the side away from Mrs. Horner, and we all kind of crowded into the frame of the arched doorway at the landing, it being the strongest point.

Now that the pressure was off, the people in the lobby looked less like water sloshing in a bucket and more like soapy water in a tub being drained out the plughole. The stream of people in the middle flowed faster than those along the edges, just like you see with soapsuds, but they was all getting there.

Gilt flaked off the scrollwork over our heads, dusting Mrs. Horner's black velvet cap and my shoulders. When the desk clerk and Alexandre was crowding the last few hotel guests out the door, having heroically—I thought—stayed until last, Mrs. Horner gave my hand a squeeze and let it go. Hilaria's too.

I almost clutched after her, but she said, "Mind you

hold the balustrade on the way down," and that seemed like such sensible advice I did it with both hands. The risers was kicking the bottom of my kitten heel boots with every step, the hotel pitching like a ship in a West Indies hurricane. The chandeliers swung and pitched, making whooshing noises they was swinging so hard now, and I gritted my teeth to run under them as fast as I possibly could. Even its guttering light revealed that the lobby floor was treacherous, littered with shattered glass and torn cloth and spilled drinks.

We was halfway down the big curving grand stair when the chandeliers crashed into one another. Shattering glass sparkled as it rained down on us, showering along with long arcing orange streaks of sparks. Some of the lights didn't shatter; those kept burning.

Clear as if the police were pounding on the door, I heard five sharp, loud knocks.

Before a cat could have jumped on a bird, the molded and painted plaster ceiling cracked and began to cascade into the space before the open doors. "Back up!" one of the Arcades yelled, or maybe both of them. I wobbled and rocked as the stairs pitched. My stomach dropped sickeningly as I felt my balance go, and my arms was pinwheeling.

Somebody grabbed me by the shoulders and waist and hauled me back up the stairs. It wasn't hands, though—it was some kind of metal contraption like spider legs.

When I managed to crane my neck over my shoulder, I saw Hilaria's corset had unfolded into an insecty chrysanthemum and the legs were what had me. More of them was steadying her, hooked into the stair carpet and braced against the balustrade.

We looked at each other for a second, while I felt grateful and she probably wondered if she'd given away too much of her bunco. She might have acted on instinct and be regretting it now, but I was glad she hadn't let me fall. The spider legs steadied me for a moment longer. Then Hilaria did something with her cuff bracelet and they zipped back under the brocade of her dress. There was a little unsettling wriggle, like she was made of worms, but then her corset was as shapely as ever. I couldn't even see the openings they had come out of. The gaps along the stiff bodice seams lay flat as a hidden pocket, which was a nice bit of sewing, and professionally I wondered which one of 'em was the seamstress.

"The spirits come quietly," she said, with intense conviction or a solid show of it. She smoothed her hands over those bodice seams possessively enough that I was sure she'd done the sewing. "Our clients expect more . . . drama than that."

I weren't sure what I was supposed to say to that, or even what I thought about it. I was saved—after a fashion—when something creaked and thumped behind me. I spun back toward the lobby. What was left of the chandeliers stayed burning just long enough for us to watch as the whole lobby ceiling collapsed from the center out. Then the chandeliers, too, fell and we was plunged into dusty, choking blackness. The staircase heaved under my feet like a bucking bull. I clutched the balustrade, which was too wide, flat, and polished to afford much grip, though it would have been ace-high for sliding down, and hung on best I could, which is to say for dear life.

It occurs to me in retrospect that I got kind of a bad history with stairs. Maybe I just ought to live out my life at ground level from now on.

———

"We must get off these stairs."

The voice out of the darkness was Hilaria's, calmer in catastrophe than she had any right to be. Someone's hand took my collar and tugged.

Mrs. Horner said, "Gently now, walk soft. Close to the edge of the step, where it's stronger."

A beam of dim light rattled into existence. Mrs. Horner held something in her hand, a sort of metal tube with a frosted lens at one end. It cast a focused beam, illuminating the billowing plaster dust and to a lesser extent the broken steps underfoot. I followed her advice, picking my way over buckled carpet and splintered wood, the Arcade sisters climbing before me.

Other than the creak of strained wood, the only sound was the rustle of taffeta and the scuff of little shoes as we four women climbed back to the relative safety of the landing. I could barely pick out the shimmering colors of the Arcades' silk dresses through the plaster dust, which caked my lashes and made my mouth and nostrils feel like somebody had spackled in there.

The building was still now, the rocking and tossing ended, and mostly quiet enough that I could hear the ringing in my ears I picked up after that explosion down on the docks last year. The doctor says it's tinnitus, which having a name for it don't change how annoying it is, but at least it ain't tintinnabulation, I suppose.

The building moaned as it settled, which covered up the sounds inside my head. I felt it shivering through my soles. The new configuration it fell into steadied, though I held my breath until it did. Then we was under that arch in the load-bearing wall, and trying to catch our breaths, using folded shawls and sleeves to filter the dust out of the air a little.

The electric torch in Mrs. Horner's hand flickered. She shook it gently, and it brightened. "Follow me."

We did, stepping over tumbled furniture and chunks

of plaster. I mourned in my heart for the gorgeous old hotel, though it wasn't past repair.

"Told you it wasn't any poltergeist," said Mrs. Horner, sounding satisfied. I glanced over and damned if there wasn't a smug little cat-in-cream expression on that velvety face.

"You don't call that a haint? It sure weren't no natural earthquake."

"No. I call it a natural creature, though. You heard the loud knocks right before the ceiling fell."

The Arcade sisters looked at each other. Hypatia fished the bosom gun out of her bosom and held it low by her side, mostly concealed in her skirts and the ruffles on her lace jacket.

I left my piece right where it lived, which is to say in concealment. "Borglums," said I.

"Tommy-knocker," Mrs. Horner agreed. We came around the corner into a hallway with the lights still on. She flipped off her torch, probably conserving the battery.

"Though what a generally friendly creature that lives in mines is doing tearing up a fancy hotel is beyond me."

Well, reader, it's a fact. I'm not always the fastest on the uptake, but I thought of Old Boston right away, and his smashed-up ironbound trunk. I didn't say anything, because I didn't want to sound like an idiot. Which is always the best way to end up *looking* like an idiot, but it never seems that way at the time.

So I just asked, "Where are we going?"

"I know another way out," was all she'd answer.

"Oh, no way are we going in there."

The redheaded sisters and me stood in the open doorway of the empty auditorium, listening to the creaks of the damaged hotel amplified in the dark, acoustic space. Mrs. Horner was a few steps ahead of us, widow's weeds fading into the black.

"There's a stage door," she said.

"If that ain't riot barred, too."

"I opened all of the riot bars." She lifted the electric torch, gave it another shake, and flipped the beam on. It was a relief to be breathing air that didn't stink of plaster dust. "There's no one in here. Come on, unless you want to still be here when *this* roof comes down."

It got us moving, though the Arcade sisters was a step or two behind me. We trooped along suspiciously, like a nervous caterpillar sprouting eyes from every segment. I went down the auditorium stairs holding on to the rail, expecting these to try to buck me off as well. I was that glad Priya had gone home and was safe—and with all the logic of a child who wants her dolly, I fiercely wished she was here holding on to my hand.

There was a stair up from the orchestra pit, and Mrs. Horner led us through it and up onto the stage past the footlights. The stage was so shiny underfoot I was afraid to step on it, for fear it might be as slick as ice. She made a sharp turn to the left. There was, I was surprised to see, layers of curtains on the sides, with gaps in between them. You couldn't see that from the audience, but it made it easy for the actors and hands—or, in this case, us—to slip in between them and get backstage.

I'd never been backstage in a theatre—or even an auditorium—before, but Mrs. Horner hustled us along right smart, so I didn't have the time I wished to appreciate it.

She led us down a kind of rickety hall with doors on either side—labeled "Prop Room," "Dressing Room," and so forth—to a metal door that reminded me unpleasantly of the hatches in a submersible. She tried to turn the handle and cursed.

"Miss Memery, hold this torch for me?"

"Please," I said, "when we're being chased by angry Knockers you go ahead and call me Karen."

She smiled and started rooting around under the edge of her black velvet cap. "Where do you think the tommy-knockers came from, all of a sudden?"

"My sister is very sensitive," Hilaria said staunchly. "Perhaps it sensed her presence and wanted to get her attention."

Mrs. Horner and me, we shared a look. Then I said, "It might have been here for a while. I got a feeling about those murders a few years back. Maybe that old miner smuggled one back from Alaska and it got loose and tore the place up."

"Then why would it get angry *now*?"

I remembered the hard, sharp knocks I'd heard right before my table flipped. I looked at the Arcade sisters. "Maybe it's been hiding. I wonder if it didn't like you ladies"—I gestured to the Arcades, not realizing I still had the electric torch in my hand, so crazy shadows spiraled everywhere—"cutting in on its turf, with the knocking and the table flipping."

"We didn't flip any tables, strictly speaking." Hypatia spoke primly, but there was a twinkle in her eye.

Mrs. Horner produced two hairpins from under her cap. "Shhh. Stop quarreling, girls. I hear something."

I did, too. A knocking—more distant, this time, and ominous.

"Karen, hold the light steady on this lock." Mrs. Horner hefted her pins. "These aren't ideal."

"Allow me," said Hypatia. She touched two of her buttons in a short pattern, and her corset handed her two slim metal tools. She raised her brows at Mrs. Horner, and Mrs. Horner stepped back.

Hypatia bent to the lock and slid her tools inside. I held the light for her, which I think was just psychological, because she couldn't see inside the lock anyway. I was interested to watch what she was doing, though, and I bet Priya would have been, too.

I weren't so fascinated, though, that I didn't hear the heavy tread of what sounded like hobnailed boots approaching through the auditorium. Whoever was responsible for the mirror finish on those stage boards weren't going to be happy when nail boots stomped across them to get to us.

Which was a ridiculous thing to worrit on when the ceiling was caving in willy-nilly all over the Rain City Riverside, but sometimes fussing over small things can make the big ones seem farther away.

The stomping came closer. Hypatia swore at the lock, and looked up at Mrs. Horner. "It's a tricky one. Do you want to try?"

The old lady crouched down and took the tools away from the girl. Her face creased in concentration as she leaned close, seeming to strain to listen through the thumping.

I heard the thing step up onto the stage. I glanced over my shoulder, but it was a yawning blackness behind us, and I didn't dare turn the torch away from the lock. That didn't stop my eye muscles from feeling like they was straining into all that dark.

"Almost," Mrs. Horner said, like she was talking to herself. "Karen, please stop flashing that light in my eyes?"

Apparently I hadn't been holding the torch none too steady. It was jiggling every time I glanced over my shoulder at the approaching boot tread.

Now there was a metallic scraping noise, too.

"Where should I shine it?"

"Anyplace you want that isn't toward me!"

I whipped it around so fast it probably caused headache in the onlookers. Hypatia yelped in surprise, which must have been at the movement, because the instant the light hit the thing coming up behind us the yelp changed to a kind of deflating hiss.

I didn't make no sound, me, because I was standing there like to swallow a pint of spiders, my jaw was so far dropped open.

I ain't never seen a borglum before, but I am confident in saying that the little man in hobnailed boots leaning on his pickaxe in the middle of the scarred-up stage boards was a borglum, all right. For one thing, there *was* the pickaxe. It had a head big enough for a brawny man, which should have made it comically outsized, especially as the handle had been cut down from one intended for a full-sized miner—but my blood chilled down my back as I remembered the murders as the Professor had described them to me. For another, he glittered like mica when the electric torch beam hit him, as if he was kin to that mirrored ball hanging in the ballroom, casting sparkles everywhere.

He was about thigh tall and twice as broad as you'd expect given his height, with dark eyes sparkling like berries in a thorny bush amid all that bristly beard and eyebrows sticking out from under a squashed, muddy broad-brim hat. The skin on his nose and around his eyes sparkled, too, and so did the beard and hair and eyebrows—like he'd been powdered all over with gold dust.

What surprised me, and then surprised me that it had surprised me, was that he was dressed like a miner in canvas pants held up by buttoned-on suspenders and a faded red-striped calico shirt. I don't know quite what I'd expected, but a tidy little suit of clothes—a bit frayed at the cuffs and seams—was not it, and it made me wonder if borglums had wives and mothers to do their sewing for them, and where they got the fabric.

I wished now I'd pulled out my revolver, earlier. Or that I was holding the torch in my left hand, because the slit in my skirts that let me get to the iron was on the right. Your mind goes the strangest places when you're staring at the tip of a pickaxe while it keeps sending gleams this way and that and a wee tiny man is taking slow, menacing steps toward you.

Mrs. Horner didn't look up, and I heard the lock spring open with a sharp, bright click that was like the sound of your family opening the door to you on Christmas morning. I felt like I'd been waiting for that click all my life. I took a step back and felt my bustle press up against somebody.

Mrs. Horner jumped to her feet, spry as a girl, and she must have grabbed the door handle, because the latch clicked and scraped and the person behind me—Hilaria, by the height—stepped into me to make room for the door to open. I should have moved to make room for her, but nothing on the green earth or in the greener sea could have compelled me to take one step closer to that little man and his not so little pickaxe, lazily slung over his shoulder.

He tapped the floor with one heel, and my head felt like it exploded from the inside with the sound of the knocking. It beat in waves against the backs of my ears. Hilaria made a thin sound of distress and covered hers with her palms, which didn't seem to help her any.

The hotel lurched, settling under our feet—a fall of

six inches that for a split second seemed like it would go on until we'd dropped into the pits of Hell. Plaster grit and dust hailed from the ceiling. Hypatia let out a little shriek and Mrs. Horner said, "Blast it!" which seemed like heavy blasphemy for her.

"The door's wedged," she said. I heard and felt her give it an extra yank, but I could no more take my eyes off the borglum to look than I could have flipped 'em around to the back of my head to peer between the teeth of my tortoiseshell combs. She sounded calm—like a woman who's spent a good chunk of her life untying knots while submerged in a glass tank. She turned in her steps and took the bend of my left arm, which weren't the one holding the torch.

She handed the lockpicks back to Hypatia casually as passing the sugar. Hypatia took them without a word, plaster dust drifting out of the crevices in her lace coat. I wondered if the goblet of ice water was forgiven in the face of larger problems.

"What do we do now?" Hilaria also sounded too calm, but I bet if I had the light to see by I could have made out her pulse shimmering in her long neck like that of a horse that's been run to foundering.

I don't know if she was talking to Mrs. Horner, me, or her sister. My money's on that last one. But I had no answers, and whatever Mrs. Horner or Hypatia might have said was drowned out as the borglum tapped his heel again and the building answered with a terrible trembling and that savage knocking that pounded in my ears like it was coming from inside my skull bones.

He unlimbered his pickaxe. I shied back, the torch beam slashing about wildly and weirdly through the dust. Maybe I had some idea of using it to fight with, the barrel being metal, but mostly what I thought was that I hoped they didn't make Priya come and identify me.

But he didn't come any closer, for an oddity. When I got the light shone back on him, it didn't seem to hurt his eyes to stare right back up the beam. He just flipped the pick over so the head was down and leaned on it, arms crossed, frowning up at us.

Us four women crowded into a line. I waited for another knocking, maybe one that would bring the whole cracked ceiling and rafters down on us. But it didn't come.

I remembered, pretty darn clear, those chandeliers swinging together, sparking and crackling and crashing—and coming down right on the heels of Alexandre as he heroically made himself the last one out the door.

Barring the door—barring our escape—but not doing anybody any real harm.

I looked at the knocker, and I said, "What do you want with us, sir?"

Now it may seem odd to call a borglum sir, and to be honest I don't know if that critter was a he-critter or a she-critter or if they even make such distinctions among borglum-kind, but my ma taught me that it rarely does harm to be courteous, and Miss Bethel ground that same politeness into me.

The borglum seemed to listen to me, though. He tipped his head like a dog who's trying to figure out what on earth those weird sounds you're making might mean, and I saw his ears poking out the sides of his dirty cap, long and curlicued and ruffled and pointed and shaped a bit like the arrowhead leaves of jimsonweed.

He knocked again, but gentler this time.

The other ladies was looking at me, like they was wondering what craziness was going to come out of my mouth next, and I can't say I have any blame for them. I didn't know myself, and was looking for it, when the borglum's knocking was answered by a sound in the street outside the door. It was a ringing metal sound, like shod hooves running on cobblestones, except it was louder and there was two beats instead of four. The sound was getting closer, louder, and I thrilled to it even as it started to shake dust off the wall behind us and crack the already-cracked paint in big running flakes.

Breathing in all that lead couldn't be good for us, but there wasn't a lot we could do about it. And a second later, the metal clattering outside didn't stop getting closer and I realized we had bigger problems.

"Get away from the door!" I yelled, trying to be heard over all the things thumping on other things.

Hypatia looked at me blankly. "Get away from the *door*?"

I grabbed her arm and yanked her to the side, throwing her down with me on top of her. Hilaria and Mrs. Horner hit the floor beside us. Something thundered against the outside of the door—a flurry of fists, it sounded like, if fists was sledgehammers—and then the thing was just torn off its hinges and the night-cold and fog came rolling in, along with the glow of the streetlamps that illuminated the stage-door entry.

Something big blocked the light, beams dancing through the gaps in it as it moved. Pistons creaked, and so did the doorposts as the machine forced itself into the too-small space, scraping and splintering. I rolled over, letting Hilaria up, relieved that Priya'd had the sense not to just come charging through the door and the support posts, and feeling a little ridiculous that I hadn't trusted her to know well enough to be careful.

She was, after all, an engineer.

Because it *was* Priya, strapped into the modified Singer sewing machine she'd turned into a suit of armor, which I'd worn just earlier that same winter to rescue a cat and to fight with some Russians.

She finally squeezed the chassis through the gap where the door had been, without collapsing the doorway any further. I expected the borglum to fly at her while she was vulnerable, or at least to leg it. The electric torch had gone out when I dove for the floor, and I shook it good to get it to come back on, following Mrs. Horner's excellent example. The beam steadied after a second, and when I turned it back toward where the borglum had been he was still there. Still leaning on his pickaxe. Head cocked the other way now, as if he was considering what sort of thing Priya in her machine might be, and what to do about her.

I got my legs untangled from my petticoats, more or less, and pushed myself up onto one knee. The work lights on the Singer hissed and crackled into life, too dazzling for me to look at Priya directly. I'm not sure if the hard electric arcs hurt the knocker, startled him, or if he just decided he might as well be elsewhere on account of some giant metal monster crashing his pickaxe party, but he lifted up his pick and slammed it on the floor by his feet, and before you could say "Jack Robinson" he'd vanished through the fresh new hole, falling out of sight with the flinders of the boards.

A hollow sound of knocking echoed up through the hole where he had been, but I didn't get close to it in time to see anything down there in the beam of the rekindled torch except for dust and blackness.

The hole seemed to go down a long way and I didn't feel like looking at it. I glanced down at my hands and then away again; I'd skinned up my knuckles pretty good and the sight of blood has never set easy with me, even when there's an arc light making it look more black than red due to glare. I still couldn't look at Priya because of that same glare, so I shut my eyes and shaded them and said, "I missed you."

I would have hurled myself at her, but I would have just been hugging the machine.

She snorted. The Singer hissed steam as she shifted her weight. "This don't mean I'm not still mad. It just means I'm not planning to let nobody else have the killing of you."

She sounded angry, too, not teasing. I figured I didn't want to fight with her in front of the Arcades, or Mrs. Horner, who was gathering around us on all sides. So I said, "How did you know where I was?"

She held up a little device I recognized. It was a locator we'd used to keep track of our friend Miss Francina this one time when she was infiltrating an enemy stronghold.

"I slipped the bug into the lining of your reticule," Priya said. "Just in case you got into trouble without me again."

I started to say something snitty, and then shut my mouth. Considering she had just come to the rescue, I guessed I didn't have too much to snit about. I thought about asking how she'd known to come back, but it wasn't like you wouldn't be able to see the whole Riverside shaking and shuddering and falling over itself from just about anywhere downtown, never mind up in the hills overlooking the city where our little ranch was. I could hear her breathing heavily, winded, so she'd obviously run the whole way back. In the Singer, that was fast enough.

I stepped to the side so I could open my eyes and look at her. She was kind enough not to turn the lights to follow me, which was good; I was starting to feel like I was in for an interrogation.

She'd grown tall enough that the Singer fit her better than it did me, now, and I felt a little spike of jealousy. Which was stupid, and I knew it as soon as I felt it, and felt even more ashamed over it when Priya said, "We've got to get you out of here."

Mrs. Horner shook more plaster dust out of her widow's weeds, then undid what little good the work had done by wiping her hands down the front and sticking the right one out to Priya like they was both white men. "You must be Miss Memery's friend," she said. "She mentioned you were an engineer while she was telling me about you. Your work?" A nod to the Singer. "Very fine."

The littler Arcade was giving the Singer the once-over, too, and whatever jealousy I'd been feeling wound up puffed over with pride. My girl's work was good enough to draw praise and attention from these other lady engineers, and that made me gloating happy.

I introduced them all, right quick and not at all formally, and Miss Francina would have been that put out with my performance. I could hear her tutting in my mind.

Priya sort of bowed to Mrs. Horner, as best she could inside the Singer, and said formally, "I am sorry to have missed your performance."

Mrs. Horner twinkled at her like a much younger woman. "Tonight's performance has been postponed due to shenanigans," she said. "I feel confident that the opera house will permit me to do a makeup tomorrow, rather than having to refund all those tickets. Your Miss Memery has a backstage pass to share with you and I expect to see you both there on the morrow.

"Now. Shall we shake the dust from our shoes, my ladies?"

But something about just leaving was bothering me, and as they turned toward the busted-down door I asked, "What about the Riverside? We can't just leave this borglum running around loose in here."

"Karen." Priya sighed. She didn't ask me what a borglum was, which was typical. She'd look it up or figure it out herself from context, and only if she couldn't would she ask me to explain. "You can't solve everybody's problem every time. They can hire somebody to trap it or something, I'm sure. If they even decide to rebuild."

I felt even sadder thinking about that. Rapid wouldn't be Rapid without the Rain City Riverside. And what about Alexandre and the others, and their jobs?

And what about the poor borglum?

I was starting to have a theory about that little Knocker, you see.

"I think the borglum needs help," I said.

"The borglum tried to kill us," Hypatia said.

"He tried to keep us from leaving," Mrs. Horner corrected. "He had the opportunity to do more. But he didn't. Kidnapping's a heinous act, but it isn't murder."

Hilaria looked at me. "You talked to him," she said, more curious than suspicious. "How did you know to talk to him?"

"Well," I said. "He was real careful not to drop those chandeliers on any people, wasn't he? He could have killed us, or a lot of those people in the lobby. I think he was probably in Old Boston's steamer trunk, the one that was smashed up, and he'd kidnapped the borglum from Alaska and brought it back. I don't know how he escaped, or why he decided to kill him and everybody else, and blind the piano player, and why he didn't decide to kill us or Alexandre or any of the guests, though."

"Well," Priya said, "none of us did anything to deserve being killed over. Maybe that original crew did." She fixed Hypatia with a stare. "Unless you two have even more secrets."

Hilaria looked at me. "I thought you said you could square things with her."

"What?" Priya rounded on me, forgetting for a second that she was in the Singer and turning so fast she overbalanced herself and had to take a quick step to keep from tumbling into and probably through the wall.

"Let's fight later," I suggested, with a glance at the audience.

She glared at me but simmered down. Or maybe I should say seethed more quietly.

I said, "It was Priya and my table he decided to flip. So I wondered if he was, you know. Trying to get our attention."

Priya was still huffing through her nose like she wanted to paw and stamp and she bit off her words, but her voice was pretty level when she said, "Why *our* table?"

Hypatia said, "Because we're women?"

Priya didn't say anything else, but she was listening so

hard her harness creaked.

"Women in a mine is supposed to be unlucky, because the borglums don't like 'em. Don't like us." I shrugged. "Course, it's men that say that, and they say all kinds of things that mostly serve to keep women out of jobs. We're supposed to be unlucky on ships, too, come to think of it."

"You and I were unlucky for Captain Nemo," Priya pointed out, from amid the rattle and hiss of the sewing machine.

"That weren't nobody's fault but his own." Our eyes caught on each other's in the splash light from the electric torch, and a bubble of hope pressed my heart up, which was the first time in hours it had felt like it wasn't somewhere down in my bowels.

"Maybe he likes fellow tricksters," Mrs. Horner said. For a moment, I thought she was talking about our old friend Captain Nemo, but then I realized she probably meant the borglum. I guess if he weren't immediately trying to kill us I was more distracted with Priya than with mine critters.

"You think the Misses Arcade banging and levitating is what caught his ear?"

"It seems to be how he communicates," she said. "It's possible he thought they were trying to talk to him."

"If this . . . Old Boston . . . stole that little man away

from his home and his people, I don't blame him for striking out." Priya spoke with the no-nonsense authority and certainty of her moral rectitude of any three-year-old. I imagined she felt the knocker's theorized exile real personal-like. "We should go after him, and offer to help him get back home. Or wherever he wants to go."

"You want us to jump down his bottomless hole?" Hypatia asked, horrified.

"There are more traditional means to achieve access to a cellar," Mrs. Horner said. "We can meet him halfway."

———————

The Arcade girls didn't like it one bit. I thought for a minute that they was going to head out that shattered stage door and leave us to clean up the mess. But they exchanged one of them glances, and Hypatia nodded and Hilaria rolled her eyes and sighed, and apparently it was settled.

Priya for her part gave me *two* rolled eyes and a sigh also, but I knew what hers meant. It was, "Here you go charging off to poke your nose into something that isn't any of your business because you caught a whiff of injustice, and I'm not going to let you get killed on your own."

Which was fair. Or maybe she was serious about reserving my murder for her own private property, but that was fair, too, when it came down to it.

The hilarity of the next few minutes was compounded by the fact that nary a one of us knowed how to get down to the cellars, though we guessed there must be a stair near the kitchens. And of course, there was no guarantee all the cellars connected to one another, and of further course, we was about as far from the kitchens as it was possible to be and still be in Rapid City. So we decided to work our way across the ground floor toward the dining room looking for stairs, which was logical, but complicated by the state of disrepair of the hotel. At least with the Singer and its work lights there I could save the batteries in Mrs. Horner's electric torch, and once I gave it back I had my hands free.

The hotel ground floor was mostly solid enough not to crack and fall apart under the Singer, but we had to be cautious on that front because of the damage, too. *And* we was worried about the Singer running out of diesel, so we was trying to move fast. So it weren't quite a fuzzle, but things was a bit tense, even as the circumstances warranted them.

We was picking our way down a hall full of unsettled plaster dust, glancing over our shoulders every time the building readjusted itself—which it did, being in a bad way structurally speaking. Priya kept the Singer close enough to the side wall to scrape the wallpaper off in long curls, and I kept my eye on Priya like a cat with only one kitten. Her back was so far up that the furious came off her in waves, like heat from an overstoked Franklin stove—but the Singer was running at a nice low purr that told me she'd throttled it way back and vented pressure. And I was keeping as close as I could.

Priya might be mad as hell at me, and I might be mad as hell at her—but I was that tore between being terrified that she was here in danger and so glad I could cry that she hadn't left me here alone that it would have taken a blindfold and three big men to get me to let her out of my sight for an instant.

Hypatia and Mrs. Horner was third and fourth, and Hilaria was bringing up the rear, when Hypatia said softly, and without theatrics this time, "I sense a presence."

Mrs. Horner might have been deaf as a post, for all the reaction that got out of her.

"Someone is here. Someone who cares deeply about our safety."

"Next she'll make a rope turn into a cobra," Priya said under her breath, and it was Hypatia's turn to act stone-deaf, or maybe she really was only able to hear the voices from inside her head.

"About *your* safety, Mrs. Horner. I can feel him. He's right here beside me, over my shoulder. He has guidance to offer, if you will but accept it. He's thinking of a word."

"Better women than you have tried to work that password out of me," Mrs. Horner said.

Hypatia turned. She seemed to come out of her trance, and snapped with real fire, "I don't need you to give me any password."

"Ah. So you admit you were looking for me when you came here." The widow shook her head and sighed. "I told Mr. Horner it was going to be like this, but would he listen? And of course, I was curious, too. But still, dealing with all the mountebanks who've wanted to collect that reward has been more trouble than knowing for certain was worth."

She looked sad as she said it, as if knowing for certain—whatever it was she knew now—had proved a disappointment. That sorrow didn't stop her from brandishing a finger at the girls, however. "You're smart young ladies with pretty fine accomplishments, judging by the sewing and the science that's gone into your outfits, and the sleight of hand I've seen you do. You could do a lot more with your lives than bilking little old ladies and breaking our hearts."

Her heart didn't sound broken. She started walking

again, and she said, "If I were you ladies, I would find me a plausible young man with good hands and a convincing moustache, and I would set him up with a bag of tricks and go on the road as honest showmen."

"And be dependent on a man?" Hilaria laughed. "Not hardly!"

"Make the man dependent on you," Mrs. Horner answered. "I agree, if you could perform on your own, that would be better. But people won't show up to see a woman magician. No matter how good she is, they'll always claim they've seen better, and if she's the best there ever was, they'll claim she's the only one there's ever been and nearly as good as a man. It ain't fair, but it's how the world is set up, and if we ladies want to get by in it long enough to change it, we'll do what we got to do."

"You sound like a suffragist."

The widow shrugged lightly, as if there weren't nothing remarkable about that.

Hypatia let the silence stretch a little before she said, "The theatrics aren't real, Mrs. Horner. But the power is. The theatrics are just what it takes to get people to accept the truth of what the spirits say to me."

"And it's a better living than trying to make it as a female magician," Priya put in. I was surprised; I'd thought all her concentration was going to not falling through the floor.

"You got to perform to make your way in the world," I said. "Even a wife performs. She just does it day in and day out, because men have their expectations."

All four of the other women surprised me by agreeing. I wouldn't have thought we five could agree on the color of the sky, or whether eggs and ham biscuits was a forthright breakfast.

"Things don't always come through from the other side clearly," Hypatia said. "The channels are obscure. But—'Mechania,' Mrs. Horner. That's the word he wants you to hear."

Five more steps crunched on debris. "He used to call me that," Mrs. Horner agreed. "But you know that already."

Hypatia and Hilaria waited expectantly.

Mrs. Horner stepped a little faster. "Girls, I lived with Mr. Horner for forty-five years. We traveled out of the same steamer trunks. I built his tricks, and he performed mine. When I got too old to be his lovely assistant, I ran things from backstage, as Miss Arcade here has reason to know. I've kept his confidences for a lifetime and he kept mine. A pet name won't do it."

"That's as may be, but you didn't know Cager like I did." Hypatia said it silkily, with a smirk that was meant to imply something. "If he were going to come back to anyone, you know it would be me."

Mrs. Horner stared at her for a long, long minute. All our forward progress halted, and I wondered for a moment if she was going to slap Hypatia, or maybe just knock her skull in with a chair leg or a fireplace poker. Hypatia might have figured she'd overplayed her hand, too. She shrank back against her sister, and jumped off her little boot heels when Mrs. Horner finally broke the silence by throwing her head back and laughing like a drain.

It was long and harsh, and when it ended the widow wiped her eyes and shook her head. "It's a nice try, since the ghost-talking angle isn't working out for you. But even if I thought for a second that was true, honey, let me tell you something you might appreciate in twenty years. That's the sort of thing you young girls tell yourselves when you don't yet know any better than to believe the things a man whispers in bed—or when he's trying to get you there.

"Sweetheart, when you're my age, you'd realize knowing somebody is not just listening to what they say. And it's not just holding their head when they're sick or even just sick drunk. It's not just waiting up nights for them to come home or keeping the hearth warm when they're off on the road, either. That's romantic nonsense one level down.

"Loving somebody for real, a real marriage—it's looking at what they do, not just what they say. It's living with what they do, because what they do changes your life, too, and it's understanding why they broke your heart—or maybe even realizing that you'll never understand why, because it don't make no sense, it's just something that happened—and it's deciding to love them anyway, because someday you're going to break their heart, too, and you might not even understand why *you* did it, and all you'll be able to do is ask for forgiveness. That's what a marriage is. *Really* knowing somebody, beyond the romantic nonsense and a pretty profile and a sharp wit. Knowing them beyond what they can do for you, or how they make you feel special or pretty or flattered or smart. Knowing them, and loving them anyway, the same way you got to know and love yourself—not in spite of all the bits that aren't perfect and need forgiving, but in inclusion of them."

We was all struck sort of dumb by her tirade, I think, because not one of us even raised a finger to interrupt until she was well finished. I don't know if what she said bounced off the Arcade girls or if it sank in—but I heard every word. Each one was like a stone dropped in me, and they rang louder in my head than that borglum's knocking. I heard also the creak from the Singer as Priya stole a glance at me. She hadn't been stomping, because it would have put the machine through

111

the deck, but something about her gingerly footsteps seemed a little more fluid and a little less like she'd been gritting her teeth as she took every one.

I thought about Da taking care of Ma when her abscessed teeth went bad—the time she survived the fevers, and the time after when she didn't. I thought about her sewing up his trousers until I was old enough to take it over, even though she hated sewing.

I hoped, wherever they was, that they was together.

Hypatia tossed her long, plaster-coated hair. All the strands had escaped her fancy coif and was draggled down, and she was still a fine-looking woman. I wondered what I was willing to pay, if she could tell me that everything was all right, and was going to be all right, and that I might see my parents again. I wondered if I would have Mrs. Horner's strength of character if I lost Priya and somebody offered me the certainty that I could just reach out one more time and say good-bye.

Whether that certainty was a real thing, or an illusion.

I thought about the spider legs built into their corsets, and Hypatia speaking in tongues. I was still musing on that, and missed an exchange or two, but whatever had been said I came back into the conversation as Mrs. Horner shook her head and said, with some asperity, "Also, I know what you want, and you're not going to find it here."

"Wait," I said. "What do they want?"

I swear to you, all four of them—Priya included—rolled their eyes at me as if I was the biggest lummox in the West.

"They want the illusions," Priya said, before anybody else could answer. "That's why they tried to guess the password."

"My secrets," Mrs. Horner agreed. "Mr. Horner's secrets. You know, Hypatia, I would have just taken you on as an apprentice myself, after Mr. Horner died. You could have just asked. In fact, I'll give you some free advice right now.

"Dispense with the theatrics. When you have a stunning effect, simple is better." She laughed again, this time a merry, ladylike chiming. "You're much more convincing when you just talk, young lady. Why, you have Miss Memery here half-convinced, and you're not even aiming your guns at her."

My belly felt kicked. She was right. Was I that pathetic?

And then it felt kicked again, I realized, because I *wanted* to believe. And maybe Mrs. Horner was wrong, after all. She had reasons to hate Miss Arcade senior, it sounded like, and people have a tendency not to believe anything people they hate tell them, whether there's evidence or no.

So what I had to decide was, did *I* believe her?

———

Maybe it weren't on a scale with collapsing hotels, crypto-whatevers, or con artists, but for me the crowning surprise of the evening was waiting for us in the dining room, and to be honest it startled me more than the borglum. Because my old friend Constable Waterson hailed us as soon as we stepped through the door.

He was carrying a hurricane lamp in one hand, and between it and the lights on the Singer we could see pretty clearly. Other than the tables, the dining room was largely undamaged. But it was dark, and I wondered if somebody had had the sense to cut electricity to the hotel to prevent the possibility of fires.

I'd been in a house fire once. My chest clenched up like a fist squeezing the juice out of my heart just thinking on that, and I decided that I weren't gonna ponder it right now. Especially as Constable Waterson came forward, and plucked his cap off his thinning light brown hair, and said, "I'm here to get you ladies out," with patent relief in his voice.

The Arcade sisters looked like they was about to take him up on it, too. And Priya might have been right behind them, because she shot me a glare when I put myself forward and said, "I think we solved those murders from a few years back, Constable."

You ever want to see a man go from concerned rescuer to copper star in the shake of a lamb's tail, all you got to do is signalize to an officer of the courts you got a little evidence to stir in and sweeten him. He didn't quite whip out a steno pad and lick his pencil, but he got a real concerted look between the eyebrows.

I didn't wait for him to ask. "Old Boston brought back a borglum from Anchorage, in that steamer trunk of his, and the thing was right . . ."

". . . steamed?" Priya said.

And we all stared.

"Sorry," she said, and the Singer emitted an embarrassed whisper of vapor as she shifted her weight—but her white teeth winked in her smile.

Constable Waterson sighed through his teeth, and I reckoned he was used to difficult witnesses. And he weren't dumb. He made the connection right off.

He said, "You're telling me that all this was caused by one critter that by rights should be in a hard-rock gold mine somewhere up in Alaska, and it . . . murdered a bunch of people down here four years back and it's been hanging around the Riverside ever since, waiting for I don't know what, and now something has finally set it off and it's wreaking havoc again?"

Everybody was looking at me—even Mrs. Horner—so I swallowed hard and said, "Yep. That's what we think, pretty much exactly."

"Then how come it ain't murdered all of you?"

"I reckon it ain't as mad at us as it was at Old Boston. Hell, maybe it saw the Misses Arcade's spirit-talking act and hoped that they would bring it home."

Hypatia frowned over her shoulder at me but didn't say anything. Hilaria put a small, narrow hand on her shoulder, though, and they shared another one of those silent glances. Hell, from the looks they was giving each other, maybe they *was* sisters.

"Well," said Waterson, in the voice of someone turning words over and over in his head, polishing them, like, until he knew where they fit together to get set into a sentence, and just how they might shine. "We should evacuate you ladies immediately and send for a professional to deal with this critter."

"Begging your pardon, sir," Priya said, draping her polished politeness over the intonations that made me probably the only person in the room who would realize it was her equivalent of "The hell you say," "and also begging your indulgences. But it seems to me that if we have an opportunity to correct the problem, and the, er, critter is reaching out to us, then it is our responsibility to take care of the matter. Also, we're pretty sure it's in the basement."

He looked at her, wrapped in the Singer's armored

carapace. And he looked at me. And he looked, one by one, at Mrs. Horner and the Arcade sisters. I imagined he was seeing a passel of ladies he felt he ought to gallant. But I remembered from the unpleasantness of the previous year that while he was a by-the-book sort, he was also not above leaving a warning lying around where somebody in some kind of trouble they didn't deserve might find it useful.

"You can't expect me to let you lot go down there unescorted."

"Concerned about the damage to the hotel, Constable?" I teased.

"I'm sure whoever they're paying their premiums to in Hartford can afford it." He tipped his hat.

I weren't wrong; there *was* a personality in there after all.

Waterson knew where the stairs were, and we went down them like a pantomime of actors in a motion picture about a haunted house. The constable insisted on going first, because he had notions about chivalry and propriety and the obligations of an officer of the law. Priya in the Singer probably should have been second, because she was the toughest in a fight when kitted out that way, but because of the hazard of her cracking the steps and tumbling through we made her go last. (The stairs complained something ferocious, but held. Three cheers for good oak, designed to take the weight of barrels of wine and beer and sides of beef and hundredweights of flour and taters and whatever else it takes to keep a hotel dining room in provision and operating at efficiency.)

This time I remembered to take out my gun, which might not have presented the friendliest appearance, so it was probably a mistake. But it made me feel better. I hid it in my skirt and held on to the splintery board stair rail with the left hand. I caught myself trying to tiptoe, which was about as sensible as hanging sheets to dry in a dust storm, as Ma used to say, considering the noise our expedition was generating in its attempt upon the southern polar regions of the Rain City Riverside Hotel.

I expected a dusty and low-ceilinged cellar with thick joists made of raw lumber—whole trees with the bark still on, perhaps. I was part right; the joists were whole trees, but peeled and planed smooth, and flattened on top under the sprung floors, which explained why they'd shrugged off the weight of the Singer. But they was high—high as the ceilings on the first floor, at least—and the cellar was spotless. The supports were vaulted and mortared, but the foundation itself was fieldstone laid dry and solid. I could see places here and there where it had been repaired over the years, because drystone will settle, but it looked like the masons had done a first-rate job and there was barely a fingernail width between most of those irregular, undressed stones and their neighbors.

A locked, ironbound oaken door must have led to the wine cellar, and we decided to leave that one for last, in case we ain't found nothing elsewheres. We fanned out across the floor then, not too far apart because the constable, Mrs. Horner, and Priya in the Singer had all our lights. Hypatia and Hilaria stuck side by side in between Priya and Waterson, as far from Mrs. Horner as they could get while still being in the room.

They was still not too sanguine about this whole basement idea but had given up letting us know it. I picked the spot between Priya and Mrs. Horner for me, though I couldn't decide what to do about going over close to Priya. One part of me wanted to fall into her arms and snivel, and another part wanted to make her grovel for that wife crack, and those two parts was going at it hammer and tongs under my breastbone while I was theoretically keeping an eye peeled for the borglum.

Hypatia was the one who found the gap in the floorboards overhead where he'd plunged through. The hole had looked bottomless from above. Now we stood right under it and watched the streetlight shine in through the ruined door and illuminate the splintered wood edges. I wondered if there had been a hole to nowhere when the borglum dropped, or if it had just been a trick of the light and the mind.

Hypatia glanced around, found nothing—not even any footprints in the dust, because there was no dust to be found. She sighed and pushed her straggled hair back, turning slowly.

"Hello, Mr. Knocker?" she called, in a clear polite voice that suddenly had a little bit of a New York accent. "We'd like to have a word with you, if you have a moment."

Well. That was one way of handling it. Pity it didn't get no response at all. She tried again, and the silence—well, it weren't quite deafening, because between all the feet tramping around and the six of us breathing and the Singer making its soft mechanical resting noises, my ears weren't ringing so's I'd notice. But the silence was . . . listening. Tense, like. *Reaching.*

I suppose I should have expected what happened next, given how Priya was still at a simmer a few degrees hotter than the boiler on the Singer. And how little she liked Miss Hypatia Arcade.

She huffed like a carriage horse that has just about had it with a driver who don't know his stuff, and put her head down inside the Singer's harness like that same horse leaning into the collar. And she slid her left hand out of the leather harness that made the machine move around her and with her, reached across her body inside the cage of the Singer, and grabbed a cord that hangs to the right of the operator's head and a little above, out of line of sight and not long enough to bang you in the head when you're moving around.

All of a sudden, I knew what she was planning. And I even thought I knew why. I wasn't sure I liked it, but I didn't see any way I could stop her. I might have yelled, but the expression on her face was mule going up a steep skid with a big ol' log, and getting in the way of that will only get you trampled.

The Singer had a steam whistle on it, though I'd never had call to wind it up myself, especially given how sore my hearing got after being too close to that dynamite that one time. The sewing machine was built for factories and heavy industrial work—Madame Damnable had just kept it around as a joke. A joke that had saved my life, and probably hers, and who knew how many others'?—and being able to make a loud noise is for safety, under those conditions.

Priya shouted, "Cover your ears!" just as I was thinking a factory whistle ain't too far off from a mine whistle, is it?

I covered my ears.

She hit that factory whistle, and reader, the top of my

skull about lit up like the nose on the lumberjack at the fair when a big man swings the HOW STRONG ARE YOU? mallet. Dust filtered between the joists and floor planks, and didn't show a whit among the plaster in all our hair.

For what felt like a dog's age, nothing happened. Then a tremendous knocking sounded—five big raps, sharp enough I swear the foundation shifted. And the knocker appeared, just as before—leaning on his too-big pickaxe, with his crushed-up cap pulled down over his bushy eyebrows.

He did not look pleased.

"Holy!" Constable Waterson ejaculated. The rest of us having seen it before, we contented ourselves with some sharp intakes of breath here and there, though it seemed to me that the beams from the Singer's work lights may have trembled a little.

I ain't sure what was different this time, unless it was that we was on his turf and he felt cornered, or that the constable was with us and he was a man—but he didn't stand there and lean on his tool like he had before. Instead, twirling that pickaxe around his fingers like a Celestial's chopstick, the borglum advanced.

Mrs. Horner, bless her heart, stepped in hard with her electric torch held up like a police baton, as if that was going to do anything. It was brave alright, but a rolled sheet-metal tube versus a pick weren't no fair fight, and we all knew it. I was on the other side of Priya and the constable was on the other side of me, and there was no way either one of us could have gotten to her in time. That didn't stop me from lunging after her, mind—but my fingertips just about brushed her black worsted sleeve and she slipped past.

It felt like it was *all* slipping past. This didn't have to be a massacre. I was figuring it out. I could *feel* myself figuring it out. And I wasn't going to have time to make sense of it before we all got killed.

The knocker swung. Mrs. Horner stepped aside like a matador and actually managed to parry him. Her torch lens exploded in a shower of sparks and shards. I did something crowningly useful, like shouting, "No!"

"Get out, you idiots!" Mrs. Horner shouted. She stepped in again, the torch just a mangled club now. It wouldn't take another blow, even a glancing one. She had decided the borglum was unfriendly, and she was buying us time. And she was going to get killed for it, too, because she was an old lady with a flashlight and the borglum was a mass murderer with a pickaxe.

She was going to get killed for it. Right up until Hilaria, who *was* closest to her, jumped forward, rose up suddenly supported on twelve telescoping spider legs about an inch thick and longer than I was tall, grabbed

Mrs. Horner around the waist, and skittered backward ten feet without turning, while Mrs. Horner kicked and called her names. She thrashed some, too, but by then Hilaria had her wrapped up in spider legs as well as her own arms, and I knowed from my own rescue how strong them things was.

The knocker ran forward, and I could about see the smoke curling out between the hair tufting from his ears. Hypatia shrieked—terror? A warning? I couldn't make out the words in it—and the constable used some words ladies ain't supposed to know, because some or all of us was fouling his shot and he weren't too happy about it.

It was Priya in the Singer went to meet that borglum. She moved before he could get to Mrs. Horner and Hilaria. I missed my grab at her, too, because I'd gone after Mrs. Horner and was out of position and also it was shaping up to be that sort of an afternoon, weren't it?

Damn it all to East St. Louis, this weren't meant to be a fight. This weren't *supposed* to be a fight.

"Stop it!" I shouted after her, but maybe she didn't hear me over the clank and hiss of the rising pressure, the shuttle of the pistons in their guides. Maybe she didn't hear me, and maybe she decided not to listen. "Priya, I beg you, stop."

The borglum whisked back his pickaxe and swung. I jerked my head away, eyes flinching shut as if the blow were aimed at my own face. I didn't see what happened, but I heard the whang of metal on metal as Priya blocked the blow with the Singer's arm.

I looked back in time to see that it staggered her. She reeled back inside a ton of metal, then caught herself before she could totter into us. She braced, dropping one knee and a hand, raising the other inside the metal gauntlet. What did she think she was going to do, shoot pins at the thing?

I still had my revolver in my hand. I spun the cylinder away from the empty chamber. Then I leveled it, braced it across the butt with my other hand, and stared through the iron sight at the blur of the little man as he wheeled and whizzed his pickaxe around so fast it sang like a lariat in his hand. I had a bead, if not the drop, and I eased my finger behind the guard and onto the trigger like I was sifting the last bit of powder into a priming charge.

Right now.

I thought it. But I couldn't make it happen.

I ain't a bad shot. But I couldn't, I physically couldn't, pull the trigger on that revolver when I was going to have to shoot past Priya, and once I realized that I realized, too, that it were plumb foolishness to start slinging bullets around in a stone basement full of ricochets.

The borglum drew back his pickaxe again. He moved faster than a greased weasel, and that heavy pick didn't seem to have no weight at all in his hands. Based on that, and based on the way his skin glinted—frankly, I wasn't sure he was made of flesh and blood and not some kind of stone-hard whatever it might be. Whereas me and my love and the rest of my little basement range gang were soft and pink and squishy, and bullets weren't no good for none of us.

Priya yelped and flinched back. In that light, I couldn't have seen blood. I didn't need to. Enough was enough.

Maybe I couldn't shoot. But I *was* standing not too far from the pillar supporting one of those vaults. And I reached out with the butt of my pistol and rapped it hard against the mortared stones, loud as I could manage, one-two-three-four, five times.

That borglum stopped with his pick lifted up in one hand over his head as neat and as quick as if somebody had dropped him in a tub of quick-cure epoxy. He didn't even tremble, just froze there, unmoving. Then his head turned toward me and his little eyes focused on my trembling hand.

"Karen," Priya said, warning. And I definitely heard her, but it didn't stop me, either.

Once more with feeling, I slow rapped out the five-count.

The borglum blinked. He looked at the pistol. He looked at me. He looked at Priya as if reassessing whether she was a threat or maybe no. He settled back on his heels and lowered the pick, which a strong man would have needed both hands to swing, comfortably and with a relaxed wrist to lean on it once more. Without taking his eyes off me, he lifted his heel up and tapped lightly on the floor.

It was hella loud knocking for such a little gesture, and I blinked more scratchy dust out of my eyes.

"We're friends," I said. Knock knock, knock knock knock.

The long ears twitched. He didn't talk, just knocked back. And took a calm couple of steps over to me.

Hilaria set a suddenly quiet Mrs. Horner down gently, on her feet, and stretched out her own fingers and arms.

Out of the corner of my eye, I saw Constable Waterson slowly unskinning his pistol, and shaking his shoulders as if to loosen the coat sleeves over them.

"Quick thinking," he said, not even grudgingly. "You going to drum it through the streets like the Pied Piper, until you get it to a friendly local mine?"

"If I got to," I answered.

———————

I had to. Constable Waterson got the streets cleared for

us, and the mayor, Madame Damnable—who didn't even have to be wakened up at two in the morning, being already up and in the street outside with a bunch of aides, on account of the happening—found us an abandoned claim back in the hills about five miles, which is a nasty walk in the freezing rain even if you got somebody to hold an umbrella for you.

We had a little discussion about getting the borglum on a boat and shipping him back to Alaska, but this weren't the time of year for it and what sensible captain would agree? So he'd have to stay a local tommy-knocker, but maybe there were some of his kind in the mines around here, too, or maybe once he was on his own he could send off for a catalogue bride lady borglum, or however borglums manage such things.

I thought it was a real good thing that the only people watching us was watching out of windows. I reckoned the borglum probably would have tossed a fit if there was folks all around on the pavements. I was self-conscious enough about the attention for us both, anyway.

There goes Karen Memery again. Boy, that trouble does seem to find her.

Priya walked with me, on foot because the Singer was out of diesel. That was fine; everybody in town knew who it belonged to now. It'd get back to us. Everybody else except the constable stayed behind, though he and I had a

fight to make that happen, and finally we had to consent
to letting the mayor send a steam carriage up to follow us,
far enough back that there weren't too much noise carrying up to us. She scowled at me, but she did it.

We went back, her and me.

The borglum followed us real suspiciously, to be honest, making sure his borrowed axe clinked on the paving
stones. Every time I knocked, though, he knocked back.
And as we got out of town and up into the pinewoods, he
seemed to settle. The rain didn't bother him none, or if it
did he didn't show it. It didn't even flatten his beard, just
ran through the stiff, sparkly fibers like they was asbestos.

Then we got up on the mine, and I could feel him getting excited. He was . . . sniffing, like, when the road came
through a blasted cut, and he walked right over to one of
those drilled granite cliffs and put his face against it, eyes
closed, drawing in deep breaths the way some new mothers will of their baby's head. He picked at it with a fingernail, and damned if a big old flake didn't come off in his
hand.

He licked it.

Then he turned to me and grinned, holding it out, and
I could see it was a sharp-edged piece of white quartz as
long as my hand.

The constable stirred uneasily—it could have been a
crude knife, sure, but I didn't see no point in that when

the borglum still had his pickaxe. I accepted the quartz, which he laid gently on my palm, and looked at it without conning what he wanted at all.

Priya, though, she's smarter than me.

"That's right," she said. "There's a gold vein where we're taking you."

———————

Another uphill mile in the cold rain, my hip aching like it was on fire, and we came in sight of the mine tunnel. Constable Waterson had apparently sent somebody on ahead, which I hadn't thought of, because though the tunnel had been closed off it was partially unboarded now, and there was a couple of court officers standing well off to the side with crowbars and a pile of broadsawn boards.

You know, that borglum didn't even hesitate. He looked at me once, looked at the constable and Priya, sketched a quick bow, and vanished down that open mine shaft like a weasel down a bunny den.

It was all so much like when you get to the end of a dime novel and the last three pages is torn out that honest, me and Priya and Waterson just stood there letting the cold rain fall in our hair for a good minute and a half, staring after him. I curled my fingers around the quartz flake, cold enough that I could barely feel the sharpness.

We might just all be standing there still if there hadn't been a loud, echoing bang from inside the mine, then another and one more after that. There was a short pause, and the knocking sounded again, identical to the first time.

Not five thumps this time, but six.

Maybe that was borglum for "thank you."

────────────

By the time we got that done, we was that grateful for the police steam carriage to pick us up from the sloppy rimed road in the freezing rain. The rest of the ladies had sensibly stayed back in the hotel where I hoped somebody had found them some intact sleeping quarters and a hot buttered rum and left them alone to work things out between themselves. I was ready for nothing so much as a warm bath and a hot toddy myself and a whole three days of not climbing out of my double-thick feather bed.

But we had to go back through town to get to our house anyway, because that was how the road ran, so when we did Waterson and the driver helped us load the Singer onto a rack on the back of the carriage. Then they rolled us home in merciful lack of conversation, which you couldn't call silence because those steam carriages make a lot of noise. But I sat there inside the swaying thing as it rocked on its springs, and stared out the window at the dark rain. Without turning my head, I stuck out my hand and squeezed Priya's cold fingers. And—maybe a little reluctantly—she squeezed mine back.

We only had to get pulled out of the mud once on the way up the hill, in the coldest dark before dawntime, and fortunately a teamster was coming down with a team of mules just as we was getting stuck going up. I wondered if that teamster was out all night for just such occasions, as he made fifty cents off the haul. Steam carriages is great until they ain't, and they're getting more popular in town. You ain't got to care for them daily like you do stock.

I knowed we weren't out of the woods nohow, but stepping down the wrought-iron kick stair at the bottom of the path to our own little ranch house about broke my heart all over again. Priya weren't thick blooded enough for this cold yet if she ever would be, and my wrap was back in the cloakroom at the Riverside. So we was both soaked through and shivering—her worse than me. Still she wouldn't rest and come in until we had the Singer unloaded and shut in the barn, and she wouldn't take

Constable Waterson's coat when I didn't have one, even though I wasn't half as cold as she was, having some flesh on my bones and also being originally from up where some real cold does come down.

So I said, "Suit yourself," and went up to the house.

Even in the dark, in the rain, with the windows blank as dead eyes, that place looked like paradise in my eyes. It weren't ornate, like Madame Damnable's old place, or the mayor's house, or the Riverside. It was just a little slice of whitewashed clapboard heaven, single-story, with a wide wrap porch to keep the rain off, and a breezeway to the barn. I felt as house-proud as Tom Sawyer's aunt Polly every time I looked at it, and right now that pride came with a busted-up ache inside.

What if all this good I'd finally found—what if it went away? I had plans to cable up to Hay Camp and see if my good mare Molly was still with the friend I'd left her with. And I had another filly coming up from the Indian Country, if another friend got his mustang mare in foal and managed to get a girl colt out of her. That was the foundation of a little band of mares of our own right there, and that was the foundation of a future.

Had we broken it all already, before we'd even managed a start?

I left my soaked shoes on the porch, and nearly shucked out of my dress and shawl right there, too, but I didn't want to scare the horses—and by "horses" I mean the constables, on account of the carriage being steam.

I went inside and got ready for bed, and left the kettle hot for Priya, but by the time she came in I was fast asleep and we never got to have it out in an argument the way I figured we probably needed to.

———

We went to the magic show the next night. Which was that same night, because we'd gone to bed with the rising sun. We arrived quite early, before the crowds, as instructed, and had to show the ushers at the door our backstage passes for admittance, because the opera house was still closed to the public for several hours.

I didn't know what sort of conversations Mrs. Horner and the Arcade sisters had had after we left the night before, but I confess I was a mite surprised to find Hilaria and Hypatia in the lobby. They had changed their dresses and fixed up their hair and looked, if possible, even more the thing than they had the night before.

They'd patently been waiting for us, and greeted us with smiles. Hilaria stood back a little, which seemed to be her way, and smiled when I thanked her for saving me a nasty tumble down the stairs the night before. Hypatia took Priya's hand and was sweet as butter to her, and

Priya was guarded and polite.

Then they showed us backstage, where Mrs. Horner was already hard at work. She wasn't dressed for the stage yet, because she was wearing little Chinese slippers and a man's flannel trousers held up with button-on suspenders, over a calico work shirt. That was all we could see of her, too, because she was lying on her back on a plywood plank with skate wheels screwed to the bottom, and her head and hands was completely concealed under something that bore a real resemblance to a big, black cannon.

The Arcade sisters being there was a peace offering—from Mrs. Horner to them, and from them to Mrs. Horner—and we all knowed it. On the other hand, almost dying together does sort of cement a relationship.

"Mrs. Horner," Hilaria said, and Mrs. Horner rolled out from under the—it was definitely—a cannon. Her hair was just braided and pinned up. She levered herself up, pretty spry for a woman of sixtyish, and wiped her hand on a rag before holding it out. There was still lampblack smutched all around her nails, but Priya didn't care and honestly I was used to hands that looked like that, though I made Priya use the nail brush before she sat down to dinner.

Priya was polite enough to introduce herself before she crouched down to examine how the cart was put together, and I knew we'd have one in the barn by tomorrow after lunch, depending on if Priya had to go into town to get parts. I made a note to myself to hide my skates. And find my roller skate key.

I started to think about whether or not she'd be staying with me long enough to even want to steal those skates, and instead I made myself wonder if Priya would like to learn how to skate. It didn't get cold enough in Rapid to make ice you could trust for ice skating, which I used to love. But roller skates are all right, I guess. Not as good, but better than nothing. Priya could probably improve on 'em if she wanted to.

She'd wandered away a step and was inspecting a sort of armature that looked like the Singer's lighter, showier cousin. It was enameled in curlicued red and gold, like a show carriage, and had rhinestones at the joints. Those expensive ones, that glitter more than real diamonds. She looked from the cannon to the carapace and back again, and said, "You cannot catch a cannonball in this."

Mrs. Horner smiled. Hypatia was right there beside her, crouched down inside the swell of her skirts, head tilted. She touched the thing's gauntlets, delicate laceries of decorative metal, and said, "She's right, you know."

"That's why we call it a trick," Mrs. Horner said with a smile.

"Wait," I said. "*Who's* going to catch a cannonball?"

"Why," said Mrs. Horner, *ingénue* as a fifty-dollar parlor lady in pigtails and a white pinafore, "my dear Karen. Your lovely Priya is. If she's brave enough."

───────────

I ain't gonna tell you how the trick works exactly, because it's Mrs. Horner's trick to keep as secret or sell to other magicians as she sees fit. I will tell you that the armature, once they laced Priya into it, was nine-tenths stage costume and one-tenth mechanism. Also, Mrs. Horner gave Priya a stage dress, so as her coat wouldn't be ruined. Priya fussed about wearing skirts, but as Mrs. Horner pointed out, she needed someplace to keep the cannonball.

"You can keep your trousers on under," Mrs. Horner said. And that settled that nicely.

The dress had panels front and back on the bodice that was just basted in so they could be picked out fast and replaced for the next day, and by the time Priya had it on and fitted, Hilaria was making noises around a mouthful of pins about how to do it better. Those two's as bad as Priya and me when it comes to not letting well enough alone, I tell you.

The cannon is a trick cannon with a trap at the bottom, so the cannonball never actually hits you. Unless the trap doesn't work, in which case you die like you was on a battlefield, so there is some risk to it.

Priya seemed to think it was marginal. Me, I chewed my lip and checked it three times myself, though honestly I couldn't have told if it was working right or if Mrs. Horner meant to murder us all. *My* job, which I was much better suited to, was to lead the pale gray pony that drew the cannon out onstage, and make sure he looked pretty and prancing. He was a sweet little thing at thirteen hands and had some Arab in him, enough to make him dish-faced and give him elf ears but not enough to make him fractious. His name was Gremlin, which seemed a little close to the bone given how I'd spent the previous evening, but we made friends fast, though he was deaf as a post, which as you imagine was an asset in his line of work.

So you all, gentle readers, have probably heard of the illusion magicians call the Bullet Catch. It's supposed to be the most dangerous illusion of all, because even though—surprise—they ain't catching a real bullet in their teeth (I know, you coulda knocked me over with a feather also) things go wrong, and mistakes get made, and real guns really kill people. And you can kill somebody with a blank, which a lot of folks don't know, but my da taught me to be even more careful around blank cartridges than loads.

So one way the Bullet Catch can work is that a member of the audience marks a bullet and the case, which the magician's assistant takes and puts into a revolver. Or appears to; really she palms it and transfers it to the magician. And it's a trick round, see—the bullet just slides out of the casing, so the casing goes into the pistol and the bullet gets slipped into the magician's mouth.

The magician goes to one end of the stage. The assistant goes to the other. A glass pane is between them, or a sheet of rice paper, which is supposed to prove the bullet's path.

There's a drumroll and a moment of silence and the assistant fires the gun. The paper shreds, the glass shatters, and the magician fishes the bullet out of his teeth and holds it up. Possibly with a bit of stage blood for flourish, because some of 'em like the gore. Me, I think I'd avoid that show, because even if I know it ain't real blood, my stomach still feels like I swallowed a boa constrictor if I have to look at it.

You don't want to know about the time me and some of the girls went to see *Titus Andronicus*. They thought it was pretty funny. I think they could have warned me.

Anyway, when the audience inspects the cartridge and the bullet they find they're both the marked ones. And there's that shattered glass, showing the bullet's course. Which of course is done with a little black powder flash, or just by making sure that the assistant fires the pistol from close enough that the muzzle flash can break sugared glass, or shred thin paper. That's got the benefit, according to my old paying beau, of protecting the magician. You can still get hit by flying shards, but it stops any spark, or fragment of casing.

Simple enough, once you work out all the gadgets and the sheer skill to make the audience look where you want and see what you want, and of course the sleight of hand. Which ain't easy; I tried some of it, with my illusionist laughing at me.

So here was Cager Horner's signature trick: now do it with a cannonball.

You can see a cannonball. And you sure as hell can't palm one.

———

Mrs. Horner, since she was pretending not to be an illusionist and all—just presenting her dead husband's tricks, as was proper for a widow—never touched that cannonball. She had four Beautiful Assistants, which was quite a step up; she told us that in previous engagements she'd done the catch herself, with an audience member acting as volunteer and her stagehand—who was also her valet, John—under the traps making the real magic happen. That was the role she used to play herself, she said, when her husband was alive, and after she got too plump to fit into the leotards and touch off the gun.

Now she had Priya making the catch, me hauling the cannon, Hilaria handing the ball around the audience, and Hypatia touching off the blast. She'd gotten the other girls to play a role in all the other "demonstrations" as well, but since this was only one of two with the horse, and the idea of Priya in the path of even an empty cannon making me seasick—and maybe the idea that me and Priya weren't as solid and fated as I'd thought making me even more seasick—I opted to take Gremlin back to the wings and feed him carrots and whisper my heartache into his deaf ears between his moments of glory.

Hilaria handed around the cannonball. It was an old one, covered in a palimpsest of names and dates and cryptic symbols. Mrs. Horner said it was more convincing if you used the same one every night.

I was starting to think Hilaria's stage name, if it was a stage name, might have been a bit of a joke. She didn't say a word the whole time she was managing the rubes. Her décolleté was probably distracting most of the men and half of the women from making a thorough inspection of the munitions, anyhow. Not that Hypatia and me weren't doing our part.

"So simple a mere girl can do it," Mrs. Horner said, which made Priya bristle and me hide a laugh. "But so dangerous that grown men have died! You will be mystified!"

I supposed it was better than claiming Priya was some disciple of the mystic arts of the Orient or something. Hypatia had floated the swami line, and Priya had offered, in that case, to turn her corset lacing into a snake. Those two was making me a little nervous, honestly. They was too much alike. Which was probably why I liked Hypatia slightly more than I honestly should have. But I was keeping that part to myself.

Hilaria picked an audience member (who for some inexplicable reason was wearing his Rebel coat to the theatre fourteen years after the damned war ended) to mark the ball. She spoke, finally, breaking her silence only long enough to murmur, "You have the look of a man who knows artillery, sir."

She said it so sultry I don't think he even noticed he'd been insulted. It made me like her. I got Negro friends, and no use for Democrats.

I unhooked Gremlin from the cannon and moved him back behind it, then laced him into the reversed harness to brace the rebound. I made sure I was on the side away from the audience, though keeping my face businesslike, which I had some practice on. Hilaria brought the ball back and loaded it, with a powder charge. She winked at me as she slid the ramrod home. My heart did a trip-hammer in my chest. She was so smooth, I couldn't see if she triggered the trap.

God, Hilaria and Hypatia wouldn't hurt Priya, would they? The Arcade sisters had no reason.

. . . not unless they thought she was in line for a job with Mrs. Horner, and they wanted that job for themselves.

I hid my face in the pony's silken neck, which was probably good theatre, and kept me from shooting my dinner across the footlit boards. I heard the squeak of a felt-tipped fountain marking pen, and Mrs. Horner saying, "I'll draw these two targets, here and here. One goes on this beautiful young woman's back. The other, she will hold between her hands. No, right over the heart, dear. I hope you don't mind a little blood. Hypatia, just roll that pane of glass into place please?"

The audience laughed, a nervous titter. Mrs. Horner had her dotty grandmother impersonation precisely right.

"Now face away from the cannon, dear."

I could not look. And I had to.

I knew my paint was streaked when I pulled my face away from Gremlin's neck, because I could see the rouge, lipstick, and mascara all over his silver hide. It was away from the audience, though, so it didn't matter. I'd just keep my face behind him.

As if he understood my thoughts, he tossed his head,

making the bright-dyed ostrich feathers on his headstall shiver.

I watched Priya turn her back on me. The crudely drawn paper target between her shoulders fluttered.

Hypatia produced a bit of slow match from a pot she had been hiding in her décolletage for no good reason excepting showwomanship. I hoped it was well insulated. She held it high when the drumroll started, and with a flourish as the silence fell she lowered it to the touch hole. Gremlin, no fool, leaned back against the traces.

There followed an enormous roar.

Flame leaped from the bore and the cannon lunged back. The sugared glass shattered. I thought I saw—me, who was supposed to know how the trick worked now—the shadow of the cannonball.

I might have screamed, but if I did it was lost in the roar.

Gremlin took the blow; one step, and the spasm of flexed muscle along his haunches and loins. I soothed his neck automatically.

Nothing could have soothed me.

My Priya staggered, and my heart staggered with her.

And then Mrs. Horner caught her elbow, and steadied her. She reached around Priya and made a peeling gesture, and I saw her turn to the audience and hold two paper targets high. They fluttered in the middles: holed through the center, each of them. And then Priya turned, too, in her enameled, glittering, rhinestone-encrusted stage dress of an armature. She extended her hands over her head.

Between them, I saw the marked cannonball.

I gave Gremlin his sugar, and I leaned against his neck to keep from fainting dead away.

———————

Later, Mrs. Horner took me and Priya out to dinner—not at the Riverside, obviously, but at a perfectly nice little supper club for ladies across the way—and between us ordering and the food coming . . . well, you might have expected polite conversation, but that would be reckoning without Priya. She says what she thinks.

"I wouldn't have expected you to make friends with the Arcade sisters, after what they tried," said Priya, softly. "Pardon me if I overstep."

Mrs. Horner inspected the polish on her silverware and found it satisfactory. "Young lady, the advantage of being young is that your life is not constrained and directed by the accumulated inertia of your own poor decisions."

Priya seemed at a loss as to how this answered her question but accepted the conversational redirect gracefully. "What's the advantage of being old?"

She grinned. "The advantage of being elderly is you don't have to make the same stupid self-defeating decisions that same way a second time! At my age you learn not to take everything personally. Most of what people do has a whole lot more to do with the insides of their own heads than it does with anybody else. You find somebody in this world who thinks of you as more than a dressed set thirty percent of the time, you fight to hold on to that person."

She laughed, to show that she was kidding, but her tone was serious enough that Priya examined her quizzically. "Also, we aren't friends exactly. But they're young enough to be entitled to a few mistakes, and when you're their age—well, I suppose you *are* their age. Let's just say that when you're old, a lot of things seem less worth being dramatic over."

She patted my hand. "Thirty years on," she said, "this won't feel like nothing. Now, I feel like I owe you girls a bit more than that twenty dollars and a tuna salad plate fit for a nice young lady, all things considered."

I shook my head.

"You know you're both welcome to come on with me. I have never seen applause like last night's."

I looked at Priya. She was looking at her hands. I said, "We're square."

"Nothing?"

"Nothing," I said.

Then I said, "Only . . ."

Mrs. Horner lifted her velvet chin and stared me right in the face with her iron eyes. She didn't cut me no break.

"I *am* curious about the password," I said.

She laid a finger aside her nose like a Charles Dickens character. "My husband was an illusionist," she said. "He wouldn't have picked anything anybody could guess. Or even, possibly, anything like a word at all."

Priya looked at me and I looked at Priya. "Oh," Priya said, and laid her own finger alongside her own nose.

Mrs. Horner nodded. "If you ever decide to go into the illusionist business, young lady, you look me up. But don't put it off too long if you're going to decide to. I'm not getting any younger."

We rode home in aching quiet, in another night of heavy, cold rain. Neither of us said a word as we walked up the steps and in the front door. In silence I took off my coat and boots, and Priya decided that nothing would do for midnight in winter and foul weather but that she go out to the barn and make sure she'd gotten enough grease on the Singer.

She was thinking about Mrs. Horner's offer, and I didn't need no medium to tell me so.

In the kitchen I found the kettle and took it back out to the yard where I filled it from the handle pump. I let my hair and sleeves get wet, courting a cold, but I was in one of them low moods where catching your death seems like just the done thing. There was a banked fire left in the Franklin stove and it didn't take much to get it roaring. Those things is well built, even if it was an old plain one and not one of the newfangled Franklin cookers, which got everything but an iron octopus attached to do your braising and your sautéing and your saucying for you. (Priya would say, "Ain't neither one of us need nobody to do our saucying for us.")

I opened up an eye and set the kettle on it instead of putting it on the hook, because the hearth was cold and I didn't feel like building up a separate fire. It was pretty near boiling by the time Priya walked in, drenched to the skin, and started shucking her gear. She hung it up near the stove, and the wool of her jacket started steaming immediately. Water made her shirt translucent, her body a smooth mystery behind it. I didn't feel like I had the right to stare.

I gave her a warm Indian blanket instead. She looked pointedly at my damp sleeves, but I was standing near enough the cookstove that I weren't feeling no chill and to be honest the steam coming off 'em would leave 'em dry soon enough.

She leaned one buttock against the table, the brown and red Indian blanket folded and draped over her shoulders like a shawl, and looked at me seriously.

"We need to talk about your friend."

"I plain can't stand it if the first thing that happens in our new house is a fight," I said.

"I dislike the idea as well, but . . . you went against my wishes, Karen."

I had and I knew it. "She ain't my friend exactly. We just met."

"That makes it worse, love, not better." She sighed. The kettle didn't have a whistle, but the steam was standing out a mile from the spout, and I'd had plenty of time to get the tea things out on the sideboard while she was wrestling with the Singer. It gave me an excuse not to look at her while I busied myself, fixing her tea as she liked it. I'd always drunk coffee, but I was starting to come around. And it turned out the tea she got in Chinatown wasn't anything like the boiled black tea I'd been . . . well, you can't exactly say "used to" about something like that.

When she was cradling a mug in her hands, she said, "What did she mean when she said you'd said I'd come around?"

"I told her I could talk you into something, I suppose. And I'm sorry I did it, if it matters." It didn't. I knew that. It didn't stop me being sorry, though.

"So you . . . conspired against me with her. And you nearly got yourself killed."

No mention of the danger I'd put her in, of course. Because this was Priya.

"I didn't love you any less," I said. Which was laggard as a three-foot mule, but also the truth, and I didn't know how to reconcile both things.

"How am I supposed to *trust* you now?"

That brought me up. Because I weren't the first person to lie to her, and I knew that. Lies was how she wound up in America, whoring in a crib for no more pay than mealy rice and fewer beatings than she would have got if she'd said otherwise.

"I guess I have to earn it back." I swished my own tea around in my mouth until it was cool enough to swallow, waiting for her to do something other than study my expression.

"I guess . . . you do."

Maybe all that swishing washed some words loose of my own. Because when I swallowed, I had found out what I needed to tell her. "I got something to say, too, Pree. And I don't want you to think it's just tit for tat, and you got a bone to pick with me so I got to have a beef with you."

"You're nearly always fair," she said, though warily, in the gap where I was getting my thoughts organized. There was some humor in the "nearly" and I rolled my eyes at her over my mug.

I took a breath so deep I felt it in those ribs I'd bruised on my corset, and imagined what Hypatia would sound like if she was actually channeling my da, who had the least Irish temper of any Irishman you ever met, or maybe he learned to keep a rein on it.

I said, as evenly as anybody could have, "I don't like you telling me what to do, because I'm your wife, like that means I need your say-so for everything."

"But I am your wife also!" There was heat in it, and my back went up like a mad cat's. And then she stopped, and frowned, and thought for a minute with her finger raised like a schoolmarm. I just about held on to my temper by the scruff while it thrashed and spat, and kept myself from interrupting her.

"Karen honey," Priya said, and it punched me right through the heart because she sounded just like Miss Francina and I guess I never thought before where she picked it up, and I was thinking about how disappointed in me Miss Francina would have been right about then, "you know the problem is that you are too used to being on your own."

I must have looked at her funny, because she reached

out her free hand and pushed a dark curl off my forehead. "Where I come from, we can never forget that when we make a decision, it affects the whole family. That we bring honor or shame, comfort or discomfort, safety or peril, on everyone. But here, it is easy. It is easy to think I could just not answer my father, because he is shamed by my life and abuses me for it. But I have a duty to consider him. Even if I choose something different, something against his wishes, I must acknowledge that he does have those wishes. They might be wrong for me, but they are his."

"I don't understand."

"You are fearless," she said, with perfect love. "You are like the horse, yes, who has no idea that it can be harmed by the jump, or the fall. You know only that the obstacle is before you. When you see something that you think needs doing, you do not stop to consider consequences, and nothing has ever turned you back. You are the bravest person I have ever known. And I cannot complain too much about these traits of your character, because I am here, alive, and my sister is home, alive, because you saw me in need of protection and you stepped between me and some very bad men. You did not think. You did not hesitate. You merely acted. Fearlessly."

I thought about telling her I'd been almost wet

through my bloomers, but she was on a roll, and honestly I liked seeing her talking about me and happy, rather than talking about me and mad.

She set her mug down. It was empty already. You should see that woman go through hot drinks. "So you cannot see something that looks unfair happening without stepping in. But when you rush forward like a tiger"—she made claws of her hands and pawed the air, and we both smiled easy at each other for the first time in I don't even know how long it might have been—"you make that decision for all of your friends, too, and everyone around you. And you do not take the time to consider that your decisions can affect me, and also other people. Can *harm* me, and also harm other people. And that we should be consulted before you make decisions and get into fights that might, for example, end in your death."

"It's my life," I said, a little sulkily.

"And you are my wife," she answered, smooth and calm. "So if you go to jail or lose your life, what happens to me? Where do I go? How do I run a ranch? How do I live without you, Karen Memery?"

That stuck me like a porcupine spine. Because I knew just what she meant, having thought it myself once or twice. I'd die for her, and she knowed it was so. But I'd die for her in part because it would be better than living without her, and . . .

. . . and if I thought any deeper than that, my eyes stung like there was smoke in 'em and you know I weren't so fearless after all.

"And your actions, your choices, reflect on me. If it is seen by others that we are not a team that can pull in harness, yes, then I am humiliated because I am seen not to have your regard. What is a lover who cannot hold the regard of her beloved?"

I knew that feeling in my belly, and I hated it. It was shame. And I wanted to put it aside and think about something else, or maybe get mad at Priya, but she didn't deserve me getting mad at her. I was ashamed because she was right.

"You're saying my actions have consequences for other people," I said, so she'd know—I hoped—that I understood. "And that I've got some little responsibility for those consequences."

"I'm saying that for this to work—for us to work—I need to feel like I know whose side you're on, Karen. And where you're going to be. I can surround myself with people I don't trust anywhere. Only here is there a person I do trust. If you will let me."

I swallowed. "I think I need to go for a walk."

She nodded. "Don't be gone for too long if you plan on coming back." She poured herself another cup of tea, while I watched, and meticulously measured, leveled, tapped, and stirred one perfect spoonful of sugar into it. She didn't argue with me about it being dangerous to go out in the night and the wet, just as I hadn't argued when she went out to the barn.

Without looking up, she said, "Take your coat and good boots. The rain is cold."

I really did mean to make sure I weren't gone long at all. You know what they say about plans.

———————

Well, mine worked out about as well as you're probably expecting. When I walked out the kitchen door, the lowering sky was graying toward the solid slate of winter daytime, and the valley below was full of mist. I admit I stood on our porch for a bit and looked out over the city and the ocean beyond. You'd never see nothing like those lights all aglow in the sea of mist, and the cloud overhead catching the strawberry light as if somebody held a cloudy sheet of quartz up to the sun. It all looked like some kind of fairyland.

Where I grew up, if a night was rainy it was just pitch, dark as a stack of black cats, and there was still a kind of magic to me in the gas lamps and electric lights strung all over like jewels.

We didn't have gas nor electric up here in the hills, though I reckoned it couldn't be long before Priya sorted that and our whole house was running off a windmill or I didn't know what.

Assuming she stayed.

I took an old Boss of the Plains that I'd got second-hand—thirty dollars for a brand-new hat was too rich for my blood, even if it was pure beaver-belly felt and water-proof as a good tin roof, but this one had been afford-able despite having just a few moth holes and none in the crown—off its sheltered peg by the door and clapped it on my head to keep some of the wet off. Then I stood moodily on the porch for a while longer, keeping my hat dry for no reason at all except I was having a hard time getting going.

I had to take Priya for who she was. But she had to take me for who I was, too. And I guess we kind of also had to knock chips off each other until we got into a shape that fit together comfortable, at least most of the time. And those two things had to somehow be compatible.

It would probably be good for her to go. Better for her work if she went than sitting out here in some backwater with me. She could go to San Francisco. Maybe even Chicago or New York, someplace where there was real op-portunities for somebody who could do what she could do.

And if she wanted to go, I'd . . .

I'd do what I could to help her in it. And hold down the fort here, and hope maybe someday she came home? Rapid was growing, and it might be a city to rival San Francisco someday.

Without really noticing what my feet was doing, I'd started to walk. The rain drummed into my scalp under the crease the original owner had worked on the crown of that buff-colored Stetson, running down to drop off the flat bit in the front of the brim in a steady stream. My neck stayed dry. It was a real good hat.

I decided to walk back along the ridgeline that rose up above our house. It was away from Rapid, but there was only trees on some bits of the back side, because the front side was steep and the not-so-steep bits of the back had been logged off already by the previous owners. So there was plenty of light reflecting up from Rapid and down off the clouds, which there wouldn't have been if I'd wandered into a more wooded part of our land.

So the barrenness helped me, but still—if it had been up to me, I wouldn't have logged it out. I liked the trees, and they helped hold the ground together. I should go cut a bunch of blackberry canes once it warmed up a little and stick them in the ground there where they might bramble up and kind of steady the slope there. It was getting pretty badly gullied.

Well, I got up the hill all right, and I turned around

and looked back down at the city, and our little ranch below, and the roil of mist that was the Sound beyond. The sweep of the harbor light wasn't nothing but a streamer of glowing ribbon, and I couldn't even make out the lighthouse on the headland from up here except as a sharp glow every three seconds as it made its circuit. You know every lighthouse is timed differently, so if a sea or airship captain is way off course they can look at a chart that's got all the times on it and so long as they've got a pocket watch—and they've *all* got pocket watches—they can time the light and figure out where they are neat as you please.

Clay mud was turning slick as things you don't like to think about under my boots, and even my beaver lid was starting to feel a little waterlogged. Also, I was starting to yearn for the warm, bright kitchen I could see below, and the hot tea and the pretty woman I might find inside—unless Priya'd given up on me and gone to bed already.

Well, if she had, she'd left a lamp in the window, and that was something.

I had just about taken my first step and surely not my second when I heard a whole string of loud, hard knocks, sharp as gunshots or the timbers of a mine cracking. The slope shifted under my boot, and I couldn't tell in that endless moment of panic if it started an instant before the knocks or if the knocks set it off. My arms windmilled furiously, reaching out to the twigs of those sad scraggly pines clinging to the bit of ridge too steep to log out even though they were too far away to catch and they wouldn't have supported my weight for as long as it takes a bull to buck off a kitten even if I did manage to grab 'em.

Your body does what your body's gonna do, under those-like circumstances.

Then I felt the whole clay slope give way under me, and I was riding a landslide down. And that's where I proved for good and all that I grew up riding half-broke what-you-have-'ems, and that my da taught me right.

Reader, I held on to my hat.

———————

That mudslide tried to buck me off, too, but I stayed with it. I got my heels dug in and crouched back and just tried to stay upright, while every bounce and judder sent jags of pain through my bruised-up fajitas. I'm not sure if the corset I was still wearing from the evening out helped me or hindered me in staying plumb; the whalebone sure didn't do my floating ribs no favors.

Collapsing down a hill at a high rate of speed weren't that landslide's only trick when it came to tossing an in-adequately serious wrangler, though. It threw some rocks at me, too—fast-moving and bouncing high, though none bigger than a big apple—and one or two of those made contact. It also liquefied under me, like when you're standing on the beach where the surf comes in and you can feel the sand just sinking away under your feet every time the water comes and goes.

I didn't think about that then, though. Here's what I thought about, in order, though not in words exactly:

Stay up. Stay up. Keep your hands free. Stay up. Duck! Ow. Stay up. Oh, not the tree. Stay up. I ain't staying—

I felt myself going over, the mud on my left side sliding faster than the mud on my right. The slurry of god-knows-what was up around my thighs by then, pulling me around, and my bad hip—well, you probably know what it feels like when a half-healed hurt gets cranked around like that. I ain't ashamed to say I screamed like there was no tomorrow, so loud I heard the echoes bouncing off rocks and raindrops and pine trees and probably the rocky shore of the Celestial Empire for all I know.

I'd have died then, in the mud and the rain and the dark, except that was when the landslide stopped. Not all of a sudden, but sort of trickling off, slowing down and then grinding to a halt. I whimpered. I was still, left-handed, holding on to my hat.

I just stood there—hung there, really, by my imprisoned legs on a cattywampus slant—for a long few minutes, panting and trying to wipe the mud off my face and out of my eyes with a hand that was just as muddy and mostly good for making things worse. I was so shook it took me until my heart started to slow from a dead run down to a nice stately gallop before I realized that my left hand was clean, having been elevated and protected by my hat brim, and also washed well in the rain that was trickling down my upturned sleeve right into my armpit, if you don't mind me being indelicate. So I wiped mud out of my eyes and flicked it away and rinsed my fingers in the rain, and repeated the process a few times until I could almost see again.

About then I realized I was alive, and I had to have a long stern talk with myself about the unsuitability of hysterics in young ladies as who is still in peril of their lives before I could begin to come up with a plan on how to go on. I was helped in soothing myself by all the damned questions in my head, however.

I'd heard the tommy-knocker, plain as day, right before or as the landslide started. Had he caused it? Had he been trying to warn me? Was he still out there somewhere with that damned big axe? Was the mudslide likely to start up again, with his help or without it?

I hadn't felt a tremor at all. It was possible that I had caused the whole thing myself, with my own stupid clambering about on an unstable slope in a driving rain that hadn't let up in half a week if not longer.

In any case, I felt a real permutation that I ought to get myself *off* that said unstable slope before it unstabled up again.

Oh good goddarnit, what is Priya going to think when I don't come home?

I couldn't think about it like that or I was going to start crying. Instead, I had to think like I was going to stagger in the door caked in mud and exhausted and get yelled at good for being out all night.

I tried lifting up the leg that weren't screaming at me, and it was like pulling against a rod cast in cement. You know how if you stick your foot in something, mulch you're shoveling or a big pile of seed corn or wet sand at the beach or what have you, when you pull it out there'll be resistance, sure, but you'll be able to feel the little particles of whatever moving on your skin a bit, shifting around like as you put the traction on 'em?

Well, there weren't none of that. The mud around my legs had gone from being so liquid as to be unsettling to hardening up until it might as well have been all cold, hard metal. Even when I wrapped both hands around my own thigh and pulled at it, not so much as a grain of silt shifted. And the moving and struggling made my twisted hip hurt even more, a long swell of pain every time I strained against it.

I didn't think I'd dislocated it again, at least. But it was surefire letting me know it existed. So I twisted in such a way as to put as little strain on it as possible—which made my other hip unhappy, but that hip just got unhappy, not nail-spitting mad—and tried to think my way out of this.

Priya might come looking for me once the sun was up, and she might find me if she did. Or she might not. Maybe she'd think I'd lit out after all, and that broke my heart to contemplate.

I could try shouting some more, but I was on the back side of a ridge from the town and from our house, both, so line of sight was broken and sound might not carry. It bounced around funny out here anyway, and might lead any rescuers right off a cliff.

On the other hand, I realized, I was really starting to shiver. Half-buried in the cold earth, with both it and the cold rain leaching warmth out of me ... I might just be dead before morning. Or past reviving, anyway.

"Dammit," I said. I cast about, mostly feeling because it was dark, hoping to find something flat and strong with which to dig. A bit of slate, some planed lumber, anything. If nothing else, the work would help keep me warm.

What I found was splintered branches, round jumbled

stones, and mud packed so tight it might as well have been stone. A tree limb with a sharp end was my best bet—the Indian women dig for roots and rabbit nests and so on with those—but after a while of trying to break the closest one to a useful length I remembered I was still carrying around a chunk of quartz the right size for my hand with a sharp-chipped edge. I was just hefting it when I heard, much softer than before, five little knocks like midnight taps on a bedroom door.

I looked up, and there was my borglum, standing on top of the mudslide and glittering like stardust in the rain and dark. He had his pickaxe over his shoulder, and his beard was all bristled and full of rain, and with me a third buried as I was he was tall enough to look me in the eye.

He regarded me and I regarded him. Slowly, as if I were moving in front of a nervous cat, I took my hand off the chunk of quartz out of concern that it might have looked as if I were reaching for a weapon. He, in turn, set his pickaxe down on the ground and took his hand off the haft. It stayed standing upright, being heavy at the bottom, and he took a step away from it.

"Howdy," I said, after we'd stared at each other for a mayfly's lifetime. "My name is Karen."

He leaned forward from his toes, in a way I don't think any human except maybe a trained dancer could do, and stared me right in the face from a few inches away. I held as still as if a catamount was checking me over, arms at my sides, probably forgetting about breathing. He smelled pleasant, like cool caves, like stones in the rain.

He put one stone-hard finger against my chest.

"Karen," I said one more time. I wanted to shift around to face him more directly, but of course my lower half was stuck where it was stuck, so I just twisted from the waist and tried to ignore the hip and corset twinges.

He reached down beside me and picked up that chunk of quartz. Held it up between us, leaning back a little to make room. Looked at the quartz, looked at me, then held the stone significantly to his forehead before dropping it between us.

I remembered Mrs. Horner putting her finger beside her nose. Not all talk is in words, now is it?

"Is that your name?" I asked him, words that didn't seem to make any sense. So I touched my chest again, and said, "Karen."

He bounced a little on his toes. Maybe that was borglum for a nod.

I reached down, picked up the stone, and touched it against my temple under the hat. Then I touched his chest. That was like poking rock as well.

Now he got real het up, wavering back and forth as if in a strong wind. I did it a few more times, as if to prove I got it, and he started to calm down. We wound up standing there grinning at each other like a couple of idiots while the rain numbed my fingers and my teeth started chattering with cold.

Head Stone? Stone Crazy? Rock Crystal? Rock Steady? Rock Smart? Rock Mind? Rock Will? Rock Head, like me in dealing with Priya?

I wondered how I would say his name out loud, if I really understood it. Heck, maybe his name was Rocks Remember and we were good as namesakes.

Rocks remember. Do rocks regret things?

"I want to go home, please," I said, very softly, and knocked five times on the hard, wet ground.

———————

He dug me out with his pickaxe, and the less said about that the better, though he was so good with that tool he got it done in a matter of minutes and a flurry of swings and never came close to touching me at all.

He helped me out of the mud and let me lean on him until I knew I could still walk—or limp, at least—and nothing was busted. And then he let me lean on his shoulder on one side and use his pick for a walking stick on the other all the long way home.

He left me at the bottom of the porch, and after I'd hauled myself up the three steps by main force of will I turned around to bid him good night and he was gone.

———————

And that was how I got home from my not-gone-too-long walk, and found no Priya awake, but a lamp burning on the pastry stone on the kitchen table where it couldn't splash and burn anything. That caution, so like my Priya.

———————

I took off my mud-stiff clothes on the porch, because I couldn't get any colder and there weren't nobody around to gawp at what half of Rapid's already seen anyway.

Then I went inside and wiped myself down with a washcloth and a pail of water she'd set by the fire to keep warm. My hair, for a wonder, had stayed braided up and pretty well clean and dry under the hat. I had stopped shaking with cold, but I was trembling with exhaustion when I finally dragged myself away from the split-log sawhorse bench in the inglenook and stumbled off to bed with Priya. She was warm and I was cold, and she didn't pull away. I was trying to decide if I should wake her up to tell her I nearly died again—twice in two nights, and you know that ain't even a personal record—when I fell sound asleep against her back, and I don't think either of us stirred until the next morning.

———————

I woke up alone in the bed, to hear her clattering in the kitchen. Tea, of course. I walked out, and she nodded at me a little coldly, and I nodded back with my cheery "good morning" wadded up in my throat like a spit-soggy handkerchief.

I sat down at the table and said conversationally, "I got into some trouble last night. That's why I got home so late. I'm sorry."

She stopped banging the tea things and stared down for a minute, then came over and set the pot and two mugs on the table. It was that jasmine tea from Chinatown, I could tell by smelling it. She sat down kitty-corner to me and folded her hands around her mug, which was still empty.

"That explains the muddy things on the porch, then."

I poured the tea and was careful not to splash her. She didn't move her hands. I set the teapot down. Then I told her about my night.

She didn't say anything for a long time. Then: "I'm already too angry at you for being careless to be more angry at you, aren't I?"

"I hope so," I said.

―――――

We sat there for a while, drinking tea. Or staring into it while it got cold, to be fine and accurate.

She stood up. She walked away. She came back. She did that two more times while I stared at my tea.

Finally, Priya couldn't take it anymore. "Karen, what do you *want* me to say?" She glared at me down her long, fine nose. We had been putting good food in her as fast as she could take it, and her body responded like a racing pony that's just been waiting and waiting on a little rein.

I looked at the patterns of grit worked into the lines on my hands. I deepened and lilted my voice a little to sound like hers. "Karen, love, you done fucked up pretty good this time?"

Her eyes was sharp with tears now, bright as diamonds. How she held 'em back I'll never know. But she laughed a little despite 'em, shook her head, and said, "Karen, love, you done fucked this one up left, right, and center."

It was such a creditable imitation of me that I almost smiled. But mostly I just stood there and looked at her and held my breath and hoped it weren't the last goddamned time we was ever gonna argue.

A big sigh came out of her. "You know what you did wrong."

"I made decisions for you without asking."

She nodded.

"I tried to protect you from a hard thing instead of trusting you to be as smart and tough as I know you to be."

She nodded again. "I'm stone mad, Karen. And I am probably going to be mad for a long time. But . . . you're still my Karen. You'd be my wife if we could marry, and that's the way of it. You sided with somebody else over me, and that felt terrible, but it's still just something you did, not something you are. And I'm not leaving you over that."

I started to cry with such relief right then, I'm not ashamed to say I got up out of that chair to hug her and then I went down on my knees and clutched her around the trousers so hard she wobbled. My fingers found the seams I'd sewed to fit her and the nails curved into them like I wanted to curve them into my own skin. I sobbed and held on to her and sobbed some more.

Okay, maybe a little ashamed. But Priya sighed and petted my hair and disentangled me enough to hunker down like an Indian and wrap her arms around me, too. We leaned our heads together, and I looked at her short black hair and my long dark brown hair sort of stirred up together and thought about how I had almost never seen that again, and I started to cry all the harder.

"You can be angry at me as long as you like," I choked out between sobs.

"Tempting," she said. Then she stopped so sudden that I quit crying and turned my face up.

She squeezed me tighter and said, "Yes, it is as Mother told me once. I can see why people could enjoy being wounded. Enjoy being the aggrieved party. It is a position of tremendous power over someone else, and I could make you pay court to me or make amends. And the anger is righteous and feels very good, yes."

She paused, thinking, choosing her words carefully. Her speech was more formal, the way it had been when I first met her, before my corrupting influence. She said, "And righteous anger gets things done. And in certain quantities this is useful. Anger can drive you to be brave and speak up, to make problems change. But I think it would be easy for me to become addicted to this power, Karen. To want it all the time. To make you feel unworthy so that you would always want to make things up to me. And I think that if I let myself do that"—she gave me a squeeze, and stroked one of the shiny little burn scars on my face; I knowed 'cause I saw her hand move, but I didn't feel it when she touched me—"I'd be just like Peter Goddamn Bantle, hurting other people to make myself feel powerful."

I leaned my head against her shoulder. She had a lot

of muscle on that narrow frame these days. Yanking machinery around the way she does ain't for the faint of heart nor arm.

She said, "Maybe every marriage faces some kind of temper, and it either fractures, or it anneals."

I snuffled. Her shoulder was all over snot where I was leaning on it. I liked it when she talked welding metaphors. It made her seem tough. Well, she *was* tough, but you know what I mean.

I said, "I like to think maybe our weld is going to hold?"

"You're still my girl, Karen."

"I can't promise I'm always going to remember to be careful."

"Can you promise to remember to try to talk to me first?"

"I can try."

I waited a little and let that sink in before I said, "You can still be angry for a little while. I won't mind."

She petted my hair and said, "I might just take you up on that. But right now, come on over to the table."

"And let's make some hot tea," I said, because I knew she'd probably be wanting it.

We walked the length of our own little kitchen, leaning on each other. I refilled the kettle from the tun by the door that she must have brought in and hauled water to yesterday. I put it on the hook and poked up the fire. She found more tea in the crates we hadn't unpacked yet. We'd been too tired to wash the previous night's dishes, so those were still in the basin. I reclaimed the pot from where we'd left it and rinsed the cold steeped jasmine tea, and she put the fresh tea in.

I thought about that letter from Priya's father. I thought about the look on her face while she read it, and the look on her face while she fed it, page by page, into the fire.

"You gonna write him back?" I asked her.

Her shoulders went up on account of she was holding her breath. She didn't ask me who *he* was. She let the breath all out with a *woosh* and said, "I have a duty to my family. And he is hard, sometimes. But that doesn't mean I wish never to speak with him again."

I thought about that. I thought about what I could say to her.

Finally, I said, "So I've been suspecting for a while that part of being a grown-up person is knowing that there's people as can change, and people as can't. Or won't, which amounts to the same thing, so there's no use fussing over it. And I think maybe a thousand percent, give or take, of the heartbreak in all the world is caused by trying to turn the one kind of person into the other, if you take my meaning."

She sniffled, this time, but she listened.

I was working myself up to a fine speech. "Now, that one kind of folks can sometimes through personal effort or heartbreak convert themselves into the other. But it ain't common that that happens, and you can't make it happen, and you can't hold your breath until it happens, and if you treat them like they is gonna change if you just wish and yell hard enough . . . well, you're gonna be holding your breath and wishing and yelling for a long time."

"I see." She bit her lip. "So you're telling me there's no hope of reconciliation with my father."

"Nah." I went to work on the fire, pretending it was to boil up the water faster but really for something to hide myself in. "I'm saying that if you've got one of them people in your life, it's like horses. You have to decide if you can work with what you've got. And if you can, well, you don't try to teach 'em any tricks that are beyond their capabilities. You bring 'em along gentle and you reward 'em when they ain't jackasses and you're damned careful about turning your back on 'em or giving them the chance to kick."

I swished the dry tea around in the pot—it was a kind called a Brown Betty, all the way from England, which Madame had given us as a housewarming gift. I liked the warm chocolate color of the glaze and the way the pottery felt in my hand. Priya looked thoughtful, which was so much better than her looking crushed. I put the teapot down and walked over and kissed her soft, on the mouth. She was still stiff about it, but she let me, and even kissed back a little, and I wanted to sniffle with gratitude.

I turned away quick so she wouldn't notice. She'd hung all the mugs on hooks over the cookstove while I was fussing, but she'd left the rinsed-out ones down.

"My father would not be flattered by the comparison," she said in that sere tone that meant she was making a joke.

I turned back and winked at her.

She said, "I think I understand. You are telling me that I cannot dictate what my relationships with other people will be, or . . . who those people will be themselves. I cannot bully my father into being other than my father. So if I want to have a relationship with my father, I will accept who he is, and try to lead him gently into better behavior."

"Sure," I said. "Better yet, let him think it is his own idea."

We'd owned this place outright for a week, and been moved in a whole two days, and already Priya'd tinkered up the flue on the fireplace so it drew like a blast furnace. I couldn't have got that fire hot faster with a bellows, once I opened up the draft. The kettle started hissing, so I swung the arm out and wrapped a cloth around my hand while I poured.

Priya absentmindedly reached over and turned the button on a little timer she'd made out of what used to be my alarm clock. If I want my bits left whole in this love affair, I gotta stick a bit of plaster on them says "please do not take apart."

She generally puts 'em back together better than she found them, at least, though you might not recognize the thing after she's done with it, or how it's supposed to be used or even what for, for that matter.

"What you can do," I said, "is decide what behavior you're going to accept, though, and not stick around for the bits that aren't in it. You ain't gotta turn your back on a pony as you know kicks."

"Even if I know he wants the chance to kick me, I do not have to make myself vulnerable?"

"Well." I thought about it so long her timer buzzed, and I poured the tea into the mugs so it wouldn't get stewed the way the last batch had. This was black tea, so Priya got up to fetch the creamer from the cold room, and by the time she got back I was sitting at the board and had an answer.

I poured cream into my mug and blew across my tea. I was even getting to like the stuff, though it weren't no coffee. "You ain't gotta give people everything they ask you for, neither."

And then I decided what we needed was some food. Because I was stalling, and I'll be honest about it. That fussing bought me the time to get my courage up for the next hard conversation.

"So. You going to take up magic?" I asked, as I put a plate of scrambled eggs in front of her and sat down with my own. I was thinking of Priya touring, and me . . . staying behind with the ranch? I wouldn't want to leave it, and my work was here in Rapid.

Or would she just leave me? She had her reasons, after all. But surely she wouldn't leave me, not after she said I was still her girl.

Not unless her mind had changed between then and breakfast.

She sighed and poked around in her food. "Well. I already left one family behind, and I'm getting by on letters."

She let it hang there long enough to scare me. Then she shook her head. "I'd miss you. Besides, I might be able to get some work here putting new lifts in the Riverside when they rebuild it. And all the modern conveniences. Bidets, Karen!"

She had read about bidets in one of Beatrice's French

magazines, and was ridiculously excited. I gave it three months before our outhouse had one.

"You know it's *still* supposed to be haunted."

She looked me in the eye and I wondered if she was speaking out of my heart, or her own. "I was disappointed to find out that most of that spirit-talking stuff is nonsense, at least according to my grandfather. You want it to be true. You want some proof that the people you love are still with you, and not gone away out of reach forever. You want to be told that the answer you covet in your heart is certain."

"Sure," I said. "That's how they do it, right? You buy in, because you want a thing to be true, and then even when the evidence argues against you, you look for different evidence."

"It is a thing scientists must defend themselves against," Priya said.

I laughed, thinking of the Arcade sisters. "That's how bunco artists get us. We know it's too good to be true, but we want it anyway."

Priya ate her eggs and wouldn't look at me.

I touched her shoulder. "But sometimes the thing that seems too good to be true is real."

She looked at me. I dabbed a bit of grease off her forehead onto my handkerchief.

"Not perfect," she said.

I kissed her. "Not perfect."

She leaned back, inspected me, and nodded. "That just means it's not a con job," she answered, and kissed me back.

When I leaned back, I said, "So what do you think Old Boston meant by that note, if it weren't a suicide note?"

"What did it say?"

"'I just don't want to do this anymore.'"

She picked her tea up again. "Maybe he really just wanted a change."

We speak of getting married or having children as giving hostages to fortune. But we're all so damn self-absorbed that we forget: we're also taking on the responsibility that every choice we make from that point on affects that other person profoundly. When you're alone, you ain't beholden to no one, but you also ain't got no one beholden to you, and that's in my mind a bigger duty toward kindness. People come to rely on a body, a body has to do their best to be the sort people *can* rely on. Or else stay out of positions of confidence. It's only responsible.

Priya blew her black-red bangs up. Of course they fell right back where they had started, strands across her forehead, and my heart fit to burst with tenderness.

"My mother says that you don't really know if you love someone until they break your heart and you decide that it's worth it to keep loving them anyway. Even though maybe they turn out not to be as perfect as you'd thought they were." She pressed her lips and lowered her head, mulish. "She *also* says that if you let them get away with breaking your heart out of meanness or disrespect, you're a fool."

My words had to squeeze past a frog in my throat, so it's no surprise they came out a croak. "What if it's your own heart you've broke?"

"Then I guess you gotta decide if you did it out of meanness or disdain, and if not you got to decide to keep loving yourself anyway, even if you're not as perfect as maybe you thought. Or try to be."

You get thrown hard and it sometimes kills you outright. But sometimes you just get tangled in the stirrup, dragged and trampled, and then months later you look in a mirror, thinking you're healed, and you find you can't recognize what you've become.

They were gone, my ma and da. Maybe they were waiting for me on the other side. If they was, I guessed I'd find out, and not having had the chance to say good-bye to Da would be like not having had the chance to say good-bye to him before he went out to the woodpile for a bit to split some lumber.

And if they wasn't, well. Fooling myself wouldn't make them be there when I followed.

Priya wasn't gone, though.

She was right here in front of me. And neither one of us was going away.

About the Author

Photograph by Kyle Cassidy

ELIZABETH BEAR was the recipient of the John W. Campbell Award for Best New Writer in 2005. She has won two Hugo Awards for her short fiction, a Sturgeon Award, and the Locus Award for Best First Novel. Bear lives in South Hadley, Massachusetts, with her husband, novelist Scott Lynch.

TOR·COM

**Science fiction. Fantasy. The universe.
And related subjects.**

*

More than just a publisher's website, *Tor.com*
is a venue for **original fiction, comics,** and
discussion of the entire field of SF and fantasy,
in all media and from all sources. Visit our site
today—and join the conversation yourself.